THE GREEN PARROT

T0151843

BOOKS BY
PRINCESS MARTHE BIBESCO

THE EIGHT PARADISES

A DAUGHTER OF NAPOLEON
Memoirs of Emilie de Pellapro,
Princess de Chimay, with an Introduction

ISVOR, THE COUNTRY OF WILLOWS

CATHERINE-PARIS

THE GREEN PARROT

THE GREEN PARROT

PRINCESS MARTHE BIBESCO

Translated by Malcolm Cowley

TURTLE POINT PRESS

LE PERROQUET VERT
© 1924 EDITIONS BERNARD GRASSET

THIS TRANSLATION FIRST PUBLISHED IN 1929
BY HARCOURT, BRACE AND COMPANY, INC.

© 1994 TURTLE POINT PRESS

LIBRARY OF CONGRESS
CATALOG CARD NUMBER 94-060638
ISBN: 096-27987-9-7

DESIGN AND COMPOSITION BY WILSTED & TAYLOR

PRINTED IN THE U.S.A.

TO ANTOINE BIBESCO

Do you remember, Antoine, the spring morning when we argued about the Russian soul? We strolled up and down the Champs-Élysées, you and Georges and I, without bothering to notice in the midst of our debate that we must be very late for luncheon, since we were quite alone on the Avenue.

You advised me to read the whole of Dostoyevsky without delay. I answered that I had read *The Brothers Karamazov* on your advice, and that the one book was enough; I should not open another Russian novel before the following winter; I refused to make myself ill deliberately more than once a year; I had hardly recovered; no, I should not begin *The Idiot* that spring.

Georges suggested that I was exaggerating the effects of my reading.

"We all suffer from the same ills as Dostoyevsky's heroes," you told me. "They are men."

"But first of all, they are Russians," I answered with the firmness that you call obstinacy.

"A Russian is just like you and me and our neighbors. The only difference is in your imagination."

"No, he is different. And to prove it . . ."

We had just reached the corner of the Rue de La Boétie. A man crossed our wake, veered to the right, passed us, and began walking, like ourselves, toward the Étoile.

On the broad Avenue, which at the time was crowded only with its trees, the stranger stared at us and we at the stranger without the least embarrassment on either side; we were like people meeting in the desert.

The man was tall and had a yellow beard. His nose was short; his cheekbones were high and slanting, his eyes crafty. From the breast pocket of his dark blue suit waved a handkerchief of carnation-colored silk. His hat was pulled down over the back of his head; his cigarette smelt like an incense burner. He did not turn, but still he seemed, though I can't say how, to be observing us through his ears.

". . . And to prove it? Do you see this man, I ask you. Well, he isn't like the rest of us . . . because he's a Russian!"

You answered, "He isn't a Russian."

"Yes, he is a Russian. I'm absolutely certain."

"Are you willing to bet?"

"Of course."

I thought there was nothing to fear. How could we ever learn the stranger's name? Already he was drawing ahead of us with a brisk step, a military step, the sort of step he would have learned in the Russian army.

I had counted without your love for the truth, which in others might be called indiscretion.

You rushed ahead. I saw you catch up with the stranger and touch your hat; I heard you pronouncing these rash words:

"Excuse me, sir; I have just made a bet with the lady. Would you mind telling me your nationality?"

The man had turned.

In a flash I pictured the scene that would follow, or rather I pictured two scenes: The stranger would be angry; you would exchange insults first, then blows. The stranger would not be angry, but . . . he would say with a horrible smile:

"Why, certainly. But first of all, I should like to meet the lady."

So as not to see what was going to happen, I clutched my husband's arm and dragged him toward a florist's. I fled, but not too swiftly to miss the stranger's reply:

"Sir, with the greatest of pleasure. I am Spanish."

I dedicate this romantic novel to you, in memory of a lost wager.

But one story often suggests another. While writing this book in which death plays a larger part than life, I remembered another walk, during which you caused me to reflect on the very subject I was later to choose for my own.

One day as we were strolling and talking under the chestnut-trees of the Avenue Gabriel, we met a funeral procession. All the passers-by took off their hats; you did nothing of the sort and continued the conversation. When I reminded you of your oversight with a touch of irritation, you did not answer, but turning toward a young man who happened to be near us, you swept off your hat with a great gesture and said:

"I salute you, sir, because you are living!"

M.B.

CONTENTS

PART ONE: MY BROTHER SASHA

I. SASHA 3

II. I SEE THE GREEN PARROT 17

III. "PRODIGIOUS BIRTH OF LOVE" 24

IV. ALL OR NOTHING 31

V. THE DEATH OF DESIRE. 46

PART TWO: SISTER MARIE

VI. THE SOLITUDE OF ANGLET 57

VII. MARIE 69

VIII. SISTER AND SISTER 74

IX. LORD MANFRED OF GATCHINA. 87

X. MARIE, TOO, SEES THE GREEN PARROT. 111

XI. RENELLINO 135

XII. "I WISHED TO DIE" 167

PART THREE: FELIX

XIII. THE PRIMROSES 189

XIV. THE STORY OF APHERIDON AND ASTARTE 202

XV. SISTERHOOD. 217

PART ONE

MY BROTHER SASHA

CHAPTER I

SASHA

THERE are Russians of Nice, just as there are wines of Bordeaux and violets of Parma. For our part, we belonged to a closely related species, the Russians of Biarritz; we were a Muscovite family that had settled by the Gulf of Gascony. But above all, we were a family in mourning; this was our originality, the first of our titles to distinction. More than our wealth, more than the great number of children and servants, more even than the mansion built by my father between a vast garden and a private beach, our sorrow gave us a sort of superiority over the other foreign families and, as it were, a personal luster. For mourning is always brilliant; it embellishes those who wear it, and sets them forth by covering them with darkness, as night does with stars.

All my childhood shone with its sad splendor;

it extended from our parents to ourselves, and from people to things, investing with its dark majesty liveries and carriages, nurses and governesses. Its severity was in keeping with the strictness of our Christian education; we were unhappy little girls who, under the direction of the English Miss Grey, as later under that of the Polish Mlle. Wzerneska, were ruled with a hand of iron in a black cotton glove.

Years passed before I learned the reason for this mourning, in which my mother persisted all her life. At first I believed that my sisters and I were destined by heredity to black and white, like magpies and fox terriers. I even thought that our black would increase as we grew older, and the areas of white diminish year by year.

Then slowly, by listening to the nursemaids and governesses, I learned that my parents had lost their only son. My elder sisters, Anne and Elizabeth, never mentioned this brother in my presence. He was six years older than I, and had died before I was able to remember. Never having known what I possessed, how could I feel

4

sorry for possessing it no longer? Still, as I frequently heard his loss deplored; as my mother never ceased lamenting the departure of her angel (and in such terms that I actually thought of him as having flown up to Heaven, and as being able to fly home again if he chose); as my parents tried desperately to bring him back to the world by every possible method, and even by the most mysterious of the methods they believed to be in their power, one morning I too set out in search for this brother I should never find, and only then did I awake to the feeling of having lost him.

From the way my parents spoke of him, nobody could have guessed that they were mourning so young a child. They had come by slow degrees to confuse what he had been with what he might have become. Incessantly he was set before us as an example. If we failed to recite our French or English lessons properly, we were told what brilliant progress he made in Latin and Greek—"and think how much harder they are!" It took me several years to realize that considering the age at which he died, his Latin could have been

little more than *rosa—the rose*, while his knowledge of Greek must have stopped with the alpha.

In my parents' imagination, he continued to
grow in virtue and knowledge; he received every
degree; he won all the prizes. Did they read in the
papers that a young man had been first in a race,
had become a champion? *He* would have left
them all behind. That another had won scholas-
tic honors? They would have gone to him. When
the first airplane flew, it was my brother—if only
he had lived—who was conquering the skies.

For twenty years, my mother trembled with
joy at every new exploit in science, sport, or war-
fare, because she imagined that her son was ac-
complishing them all. And it was not only in
strength and wisdom, but in beauty also, that he
continued to grow and to surpass us all. If an indiscreet visitor happened to mention that one of
us had a pretty face, my mother would immediately reply:

"Ah! if you could only have seen my son. You
wouldn't even look at her. . . ."

There were toys and games in the house that

6

were forbidden to us because they had belonged to my brother. An archery set with a target painted red, black, and blue; a trapeze hanging in a corner of the nursery; roller skates that we mustn't touch. . . . And in the stable, a charming white pony died of old age, without ever having been ridden or driven since the day when it drew its young master's coffin to the church.

Each April brought the anniversary of his death. In that month, my parents' piety toward the memory of their son became fanatical. His photographs were surrounded with flowers and lights; his clothes were laid out on the bed where he had breathed his last; the room itself was transformed into a chapel. Every one who entered was expected to kneel.

My sisters and I were allowed to pray in the doorway. We faced the chest of drawers, which was covered with a communion cloth and transformed into a sort of altar. There, among the vases and candlesticks, stood a portrait which was hidden at other times. It was a "photographic enlargement" and showed him reclining with his head on a pillow of roses. In this picture, he seemed very tall. He was dressed in a sailor suit, the wide collar of which revealed his throat. His hair, which had grown very long during his illness, darkened his face with what seemed the shadow of a beard; it made him look older, and gave him the air of already having been the young man he was destined never to become. His eyelids and closed lips seemed to hide a look and words that he took pleasure in holding back. He appeared to be nursing a delightful secret.

How soulfully I looked at the picture! It was exhibited only once a year; I saw it in the flickering candlelight that gave it life and movement, the animation of a happy sleep. I addressed my prayers to him. I said: "Hail, brother, full of grace! Blessed art thou among all the children of my mother. . . ."

I took the same keen delight in this ceremony as happier children did in Christmas trees, Maypoles, or birthday parties, the pious festivals of childhood, all of which were forbidden in our household because, in the absence of her only son, their recurrence was painful to my mother. Since my brother's funeral, our house had never been lighted up, except on the anniversary of his death.

I became conscious, in later years, of having watched the birth of a religion in my own family: the departed was everywhere present and we, the living children, counted for less than this shade, and we had never dwelt in the heart and home of our parents as he dwelt there, having virtually driven us out.

Our childish revolts were always suppressed with the words: "Your brother wouldn't have done it!" He was our model in all things; we grew up in the consciousness of our moral indignity, compared with one who was perfection itself. We tried on our good days to resemble him, but we lost all hope of succeeding on our bad days, which were much more numerous.

.   .   .   .

"Our brother who art in Heaven, thy kingdom come!"

This was the impious prayer I learned from my

9

mother. I repeated it with redoubled fervor on certain troubled days of our life, when the household was expecting the birth of a new child. Each time, it was to be the reincarnation of him.

A first daughter was born too soon after my brother's death. Conceived in tears, Olga was destined to enter the world with the yellow skin and bitter disposition of people with hypertrophic livers. In no way did she suggest *his* lovely features, after which my mother had tried in spirit to model this new face.

Conceived in the same deluded hope, another daughter was born two years later.

Once more, the well-beloved son refused to be reincarnated. The new child would never take his place, and indeed was regarded almost as a changeling. We stayed in mourning despite the years that had passed since my brother's death. The pilgrimage of thanksgiving promised to Our Lady of Lourdes—Our Lady of Kazan being too distant—was never performed.

This newborn child bore the marks of the fear from which my mother had suffered during her pregnancy. Always sickly, it died of heart trouble at the age of six months. It was mourned only by its nurse. However, this new death excited much discussion in the household, and by listening to the servants talking among themselves of our misfortunes, I learned on this occasion that our parents were first cousins, and that accordingly we were "not like other children."

Old Nianka, who had been my father's nurse, and who was, in a sense, the ancestor of all the servants, struck her mouth with the palm of her hand and said, "My lips are stitched together!" She knew why these things had happened. . . . But it was all a secret.

The linen closet was a sort of white throne-room where old Nianka held court. When I came there, as I often did in the afternoons to play with a family of kittens she was raising, I would find the other servants gathered about her. The little I knew of my parents' history I learned on these occasions. The old nurse would utter great sighs as she plied her needle, and often I heard her exclaim, "Ah, how long must I make shrouds for my master's children!" At other times, she moaned:

"I shall never see thee again, Gatchina, Gatchinushka!"

The stitches must have come out of her lips. At any rate, I finally learned that my father had been driven by his father out of a place in Russia called Gatchina, which was nothing less than the earthly paradise. Like Adam, he had been sent forth with his wife. Like Eve, my mother had been cursed in her children. Her son, made in the likeness of the angels, an Abel born in the land of exile, had gone back to the heaven from which he came. And Nianka was not inclined to believe that he would ever return to earth.

"Our brother who art in Heaven, and won't come down. . . ."

Little by little, I too ceased to believe in his return. From my earthly garden, I had beckoned and called to him with all my might, but now I changed my tactics: I signaled to him that he should stay where he was, in his heavenly garden. If he came back to us, what joys would he find to compare with those above? What attractions were there in our gloomy household? Olga, the young intruder, who howled and turned blue with rage, and nobody knew why; a butler more fearsome than an ogre, who had thrown the kittens of Zuleika, our white cat, into the cesspool, where they found a dry ledge and howled for three days without our being able to help them; a detestable new governess, the Pole; Mamma always lying on a couch, in a room with drawn blinds, where we could come to see her once a day, on tiptoe, and only to stay a minute, because she had one of her headaches; Papa still away from home, gone to Russia. . . .

It was better for *him* to stay up there in Heaven.

I doubt very much that other children have ever looked at the sky with the same tenderness. It was my one playground, the scene of all my games. Straining upwards with my eyes, my thoughts, I plunged into the ocean that stretched upside down above the Gulf of Gascony. Along its celestial beaches, by the edge of the clouds that were its waves, under its cliffs of azure, I ran and played with a non-existent child. Together we landed on the same golden isle; we rode the sea gulls into the same harbor with fleecy banks; together we set the red ball of the setting sun spinning in the sea.

By dint of hearing myself say that he was in Heaven, I came in my innocence to see him there. Not in the Heaven of the catechism, where nobody really wishes to go, but on the sleek lovely beaches that the ocean of clouds uncovered in fair weather, which is the low tide of those celestial shores. On clear afternoons I would lie with my head pillowed on the warm sand, my body motionless, my eyes fixed on a single point in the heavens, where hour by hour I watched the slow formation, by almost imperceptible movements, of a long, a magical smile that came from him.

Sometimes the clouds were a fleet and he was its admiral. When he signaled to his flotilla, a pink mother-of-pearl bark would come floating toward me, driven by the wind. There were other days when the heavens really descended upon the earth. It happened on the lonely beach that stretched to the foot of our house, when the sea retired to a distance and when all the celestial landscape was reflected on the firm, wet sand. I watched till my head spun round. I thought I was walking on the clouds; soon I should be running barefoot through the gardens of air in which my brother was waiting. The white pebbles, the seashells that studded this inverted sky, had been left by him on purpose to mark his path.

I was happy; I was mad; all through the lonely day I had a playmate.

These visions did not continue. I was growing older, and slowly I lost the bridge to the supernatural that I possessed at seven, but the memory of it haunts me still; it is like an enchanting melody heard by the heart without being retained by the mind.

Soon, by virtue of my awakening reason, I entered the true desert of sorrows and really lost the one I loved.

He directed my life; he guided me by strange

paths toward goals that were unforeseen; he was, though he did not exist; he acted upon me without having weight, size, form, or movement; he might be compared to the hero who, without ever appearing on the stage, gives his name to the classical tragedy of which he is the sole subject.

Thus, as a sort of introduction to the story of my life, I must write my brother Alexander's name in its diminutive form, which is, in the Russian, Sasha.

CHAPTER II

I SEE THE GREEN PARROT

I WAS now in my eighth year, and had reached my brother's age without doing anything to distinguish myself. I could have wept for shame before the portrait of the new Alexander. Our two older sisters, Anne and Elizabeth, had been his inferiors in everything—history, geography, spelling, conduct. By this time, I too was convinced that I should never be his equal.

What would they do with me now? Would I be sent off to the convent in Belgium where my two sisters were completing their education? I looked forward to this fate with apprehension. It was now a year since their departure, and the villa my father had built "to be happy in, and to have a great many children" had begun to give a hollow echo, like a shell.

"They're big girls now, and some one must teach them discipline," said my mother.

"We'll have to send out and buy them a peck of trouble," said old Nianka.

They had insisted on being too gay and noisy; they wanted to live. Moreover, they had not been branded, like Olga, by our misfortune. This youngest daughter, who was always weeping and complaining, always bursting into a rage, was the only one who found favor in my mother's eyes. In Olga she recognized her own tears.

She tolerated my presence in the house, but that was only because I walked on tiptoe and was always dreaming. Vaguely she seemed to realize that for unknown reasons, I scarcely belonged to the earth.

❦

It was a Sunday morning, and I was on the way to church with my mother, who was walking swiftly with her eyes on the ground. I tried vainly to measure my steps by hers. We had cut across the fields, intending to hear mass in old St. Martin's, the church of our parish. My father was away in Russia; and besides, even if he had been in Biarritz, he would hardly have gone with us that morning, our religion being no longer the same as his. Not long after Sasha's death, my mother had abandoned the Greek rite for the Roman, and we children had been converted at the same time. The Eastern Church had not preserved her son; she was depending on the Western Church to restore him.

To go out with my mother was to be alone with a shadow bigger than myself. She advanced rapidly, without speaking a word. The silence that surrounded her was broken only by the silvery sound of the two lockets jingling on her wrist: they contained a strand of my brother's hair and the first baby tooth he had lost. This Christian mother was a living reliquary.

We were following a moss-covered path between two banks, one of which was in the shadow, the other in the sun. My attention was not held by my mother, and I was free to let it wander where I chose. My instinct led me to sniff the wind and breathe in the perfume of the fields;

my eyes were everywhere. On one side of the sunken path, I discovered hoarfrost on the weeds and briers, a delicate trace of the winter that was passing. On the other side, in the sun, were one, two, yes, three primroses and a few daisies, the first of the year, tiny buds that were just now winking open. They followed me in secret. I have always looked upon flowers as friendly eyes: they spy on me; they make me a sign, and we exchange long furtive glances of connivance.

I am more Russian than I ever realized in my youth, and although I was born in the Basque country where the winters are mild and the snow rarely falls, I am affected by the return of spring as only a northern barbarian could be, and as my distant ancestors of the Urals and Volga doubtless were.

When I saw the hoarfrost on one side of the path and flowers blooming on the other, I trembled! I wished to express my surprise, to cry out my happiness at walking between winter and spring, divided only as they were by this narrow mossy path. I should have liked to run, to leap over an obstacle, to dance and clap my hands at having danced, but I did not dare. I should have liked to kneel on the ground, to bow my head, to gather all these glances, to kiss all these opening eyes, to make them wink, and then to see them opening again under the kisses of the sun. But I repressed the disorderly impulses I felt at the sight of the tender grass. I knew that spring should be considered by our family as the saddest season of the year, that the anniversary was near at hand, that joy was irritating, and that one must keep it hidden from those who felt it no longer. Anne and Elizabeth, the exiles, had been punished for being happy.

Could one ever be happy after losing Sasha?

Often my mother would say, "My children have no hearts." Uneasily, I would try to hear my own at night, when everything was quiet in the house.

I kept back the joy that was rising within me that morning like an intoxicating vapor. I knew that I had a heart, because it was breaking.

We had left the sunken path, and were approaching a dreary tract of land divided into building lots and bristling with signboards on which I read: For Sale. There were a few newly constructed villas, each standing in a square plot of gravel and crushed brick. It was from one of these ugly new houses, where bedclothes were hung out to air from the open windows, that just as we were passing by, a green parrot came soaring. He appeared to me in full flight, swift, gleaming, his wings outspread, like an angel with a beak, like a green eagle swooping down on me; and he corresponded so exactly to the picture I had formed of a messenger from the skies that I was hardly able to breathe. After circling over my head for a moment, he came to rest on the little beaver muff I carried. I had been chosen by God!

At this moment I felt something that was new to my life: happiness. And I accepted the prodigy as a matter of course, for those who have been favored with a miracle lose the power of being surprised. My mother was a witness of this annunciation; she saw my ecstasy; and even in her grief, she could not help smiling at the winged visitor I carried on my muff. I tottered under my delightful burden.

A woman had approached us. Without looking at her, I knew that she had come to take away the bird. I did not try to defend it against her, nor did it object to being taken. She seized it with both hands as if it were only a fat, docile pigeon.

"It's tame," she said.

Their voices muffled as in a dream, the two women had opened a conversation.

"No, Madam, it is not for sale," the stranger said.

"For Sale, For Sale," echoed the signs that surrounded us on all sides. The earth is for sale, but one cannot buy Heaven.

Did my mother believe, for the moment, that she could purchase my happiness?

CHAPTER III

"PRODIGIOUS BIRTH OF LOVE"

LOVE at first sight, the *coup de foudre*. . . . Neither the wildest nor the wisest of the remarks I was later to hear on this burning question were destined to surprise me in the least. I was both credulous and forewarned. I knew all about passion, though my marriage was completely unromantic, and though I had the reputation of never falling in love. I had only to think of the green parrot to understand the truth of the improbable words that the chronicler of Verona assigns to Juliet a few moments after her meeting with Romeo. "Prodigious birth of love!" she exclaims, after telling her nurse:

> *Go, ask his name:—if he be married,*
> *My grave is like to be my wedding bed.*

Why were the mysteries of passion revealed to me prematurely, with the help of a green parrot? I cannot say. It was not until long afterwards that I discovered a partial explanation for this overpowering emotion.

"Your mad love for the bird resulted naturally from the state of boredom and emotional poverty in which your parents allowed you to live," our old family doctor told me many years later, when we were discussing the unforgettable event.

"They were letting your heart die of inanition," he added.

Children no less than adults prefer to believe, need to believe, that they are the objects of an exclusive preference. This illusion, which is indispensable to happiness, is assured to them at first by their nurse and later by their mother. But never for a moment was I allowed to think that I occupied the first place in my mother's heart: it was forever taken by another. Never did I enjoy a privileged position with any one whatsoever, and no mark of preference had ever been given me till the day when, falling from the skies, the green parrot lighted on my muff.

Yes, this miracle happened! And nothing ever happened in our family; we were the four little girls in mourning, to whom every distraction was forbidden as a matter of principle; and our life, like that of the Jews, had been the memory of a great happiness in the past. I could not even assure myself that Sasha's death, the invented misfortune that served to nourish my young emotions, had touched me directly. But now, in this life deprived of affection, empty of adventure, entirely concentrated on an event anterior to my own past, something had suddenly appeared; a prodigy had taken place; I had seen the miraculous rift in the skies through which the unpredictable future invades the present and occupies it wholly.

As is the rule with great loves, the object of my passion corresponded by a thousand secret points of affinity with my esthetic preferences, and had begun to determine them already. The bird's feathers were the color of the springtime;

he was of the same green as young grass, and I adored the spring, although we were forbidden to love it, since for us it was the season of death. The wings, the beak, and the claws of the bird were grotesquely shaped, and the angel of the grotesque had touched me with his wing; reared in the forced silence of a house where every sound had to be muffled or suppressed because of my mother's sorrow and her headaches, I loved the sound of the human voice, and this bird could speak!

He lived, which was his supreme merit and a virtue surpassing all the others. He was an object of living love, and I was tired of loving only my brother, whose form had vanished into the clouds.

Later, when I came to analyze my tastes and preferences, I found traces of the violent visual emotion that had been provoked by the sudden appearance of the bird. I have always felt a preference for the exotic arts, and in the houses where I lived, my favorite room was invariably decorated in the tender green of young grass against a dark background. My eye had kept the delightful impression of the green parrot resting like a bouquet of young leaves on my dark muff, and afterwards I frequently endeavored to create this harmony about me.

Of all the paintings I have ever seen, the one that delighted me most was the *Annunciation* of Lippo Memmi and Simone Martini, which hangs in the Uffizi galleries in Florence. When I came upon this picture, I felt almost the same shock as on seeing my bird for the first time. I could not believe my eyes; instinctively I closed them to protect myself from a joy that was too keen. The gleaming angel who kneels like a sleeping whirlwind at the feet of the terrified Virgin—this angel whose wings are as sharp as knives, whose face bears a look of malice, and whose eyes slant upwards under the crest of his diadem—resembled my lovely parrot like a brother.

❦

Ignorant of the powers of passion, children love with an immense disinterestedness. On the day when the green parrot came to rest on my muff, I never dreamt that he might some day be my own. I was wholly taken up with the joy of receiving a visitation, and did not think of capturing the visitor. For this reason, I was horrified to hear my mother putting her strange question to the woman who came to take the bird away.

Even then I knew by special revelation the depths of mystical affection; I felt instinctively that "the joy of loving is to love. . . ."

On the following days, held back by the feeling of self-restraint that is inseparable from great passions, I did not even try to return to the scene of the encounter. I believed that chance would no longer be in my favor. And the following Sunday, as it happened, the first services were held in the little chapel that had been built in our own park as a memorial to Sasha. We ceased to attend the old parish church.

Several months passed by, but I continued to cherish the memory of the lovely bird in my heart. Then unexpectedly, one summer afternoon, I saw him again. He was in the Rue Mazagran, sitting in front of a long, narrow shop that was plunged into deep obscurity by a great red awning. My true love appeared to my ravished eyes. He was chained to a perch, and this time he was for sale!

CHAPTER IV

ALL OR NOTHING

I was alone with Aunt Alix when I passed the bird-shop; she felt that I had stopped short, as if some one had struck me. She turned, saw me staring at the green parrot, and perceived that I was in ecstasy.

"You want that bird," she said.

Her affirmation amazed me. What had she read in my face? Aunt Alix, like my mother, connected love with possession. Now, I can swear that until she spoke of the parrot, my heart had remained pure; I had loved without desiring anything whatsoever. From that moment, however, I felt a mad longing to possess the object of my passion. I was subjected to the torture of desire and hope, which began at the very instant when my aunt, taking the prayer she read in my eyes as confirmation of her statement, entered the

shop with the red awning. She indicated by a sign
that I was to stay outside. Reappearing a few minutes later, she led me away without a word of
explanation.

Aunt Alix, the widow of one of my uncles,
was English, beautiful, and unhappy. Each year
she spent a few months at Biarritz in the loneliness of our house, where she found a numerous
family composed of solitary individuals.

"This place is worse than a convent," I was
told one day by Suzanne, the Basque maid who
had left us because she liked to laugh. Aunt Alix
never laughed.

Like most people of our sort, we had relatives
in almost all the countries of Europe, and
through them we learned another geography
than that which is usually imparted to children
of our age. We knew the map of national char-
acteristics. At nine, I had already been taught
that one does not ask an English lady what her
intentions are. Now, my aunt had shown an
intention by entering the shop with the red

awning, and by directing me not to follow. Moreover, one could not ask the result of a conversation in which one had not taken part, even if one's happiness depended on it; one merely waited to be informed.

That summer afternoon, Aunt Alix kept the future to herself, and I followed her along the road to St. Jean-de-Luz as if she were the messenger of fate. If I did not question her that day, it was not because of my scruples or my respect for conventions; it was merely because I knew that in obedience to her particular code of morals, she would have felt herself justified in giving me no answer.

Scruples I had none when the two of us entered the little boudoir that led to my mother's bedroom, my aunt visibly determined to speak of the parrot, and myself carrying my desire as the Spartan boy carried his fox.

Left alone in the boudoir, I began by putting my ear to the keyhole. It was something I had never done before. The servants had done it in front of me, but nothing, till that day, had seemed to be worth overhearing in this humiliating attitude.

"Dear Alix," said my mother in her muffled voice, "later if you wish. . . . Why not wait for her birthday . . . or Christmas, or New Year's? You can ask her father when he comes back from Russia."

My mother had not said no!

❧

Double or quits! All or nothing! My life became that of a reckless gambler; I had all sort of fetishes and superstitions. My happiness depended on forces over which I realized that I had no control. Would I win the green parrot? To possess it was to live; not to possess it was equivalent to dying. Sometimes the future appeared to me as a triumphal arch, opening on a path that led toward Paradise—a paradise of moss, a paradise of velvet that had the exquisite tints of the bird—and sometimes as a black hole.

At night, sudden fears would clutch my heart; I climbed out of bed and knelt before the crucifix; I exhausted myself in prayer. There was something in me, however, that revolted against this bondage, against this torture of desire that had been inflicted upon me through no fault of my own. It was God who had started it all: He had sent me the green parrot; He had wished me to see it again; He had ordained that it should be for sale, and that my aunt should think of giving it to me. I was not to blame for all the temptation that had come to me; but in my heart was a desire that equaled this provocation of fate; I begged on my knees for the green parrot, but I intended God to understand that it was my due, and that having created a void, it was His duty to fill it.

My parents had recently engaged a new governess, Mlle. Vignot, a young Frenchwoman. As soon as she arrived in the house, she became my one confidante. Thanks to her, I made two or three trips into town, and was able to see my bird. Such expeditions were forbidden in general, since my parents were afraid of epidemics— measles, whooping-cough, scarlet fever, diphtheria, and still worse, the contagious gayety of the streets. Mlle. Vignot proved to be clever and obliging. Claiming that she herself would have to choose our textbooks in Biarritz, she gave us an excuse for strolling down the Rue Mazagran, past the shop with the red awning.

I could see the object of all my desires as soon as I turned the corner. He looked like a bit of fresh green turf in the sun; he shone, he talked; he ran up and down his perch, making a hundred pretty gestures that I admired all the more when I found they were always the same. As I drew nearer, I saw him more clearly, and at the same time I saw myself reflected in his round eye, a red-bordered mirror of gold in a frame of coarse white leather. I was captivated both by my image and by the irresistible stupidity of this seductive eye.

These moments when I feasted on the sight of my love were followed by terrible aftermaths, by days when I languished without him, feeling all the more famished for having once been fed, as often happens after great debauches of feeling.

My imagination was a Grand Inquisitor, a

master in the refinements of torture. It began by representing a logical series of events which would put an end to my hopes. Aunt Alix would be called back to England before giving me the parrot; my father would stay in Russia till the season for gifts was past; I should be sent to join my sisters in their Belgian convent. In any case, it was quite improbable that such a charming bird would be left in a shop one day longer; another purchaser would appear tomorrow, today . . . or perhaps my parrot was sold already. . . .

As I reflected on each of these possibilities, it was as if I were being seared with a red-hot iron. But just at the moment when the pain was becoming too great—when it was threatening to destroy the love that produced it—my imagination, trained in the art of sparing the victim for greater tortures, delicately intervened. I was burning at the stake, and it surrounded me with a delicious coolness. I was torn, lacerated, and it distilled a balm appropriate to each of my wounds; it closed them all, provisionally.

A soothing spirit whispered that Aunt Alix's

yacht would not be repaired before the end of March, and would not leave for Cannes before April. My father telegraphed that he was returning immediately. I was still too young for the convent; and finally the proprietor of the bird-shop, being convinced that the green parrot was worth a considerable sum of money, believing that only the English lady was likely to pay what he asked, and unwilling, out of pride in his treasure, to dispose of it for a smaller price, refused to bargain with other purchasers.

Once more the treacherous mirage of happiness gleamed before my eyes. Just as a little boy destroys a castle in the sand and then rebuilds it with the same materials, so I reconstructed my hope after having reduced it to dust. I had a sudden moment of illumination; I pictured the bird as being my own; and this brief lightning-flash was enough to change the color of my days.

Then I fell once more into the aberrations of doubt; I could be sure of nothing. Though I called to him tenderly, my bird flew away; he became a morning dream on the pale horizon of the sea; he was fading into the blue; soon, like my brother, he would vanish among the drifting clouds.

The shooting pains of renewed hope soon followed the bitter anguish of disappointment.

"Do not hope; hope is a bird of prey. . . ."

*

Aunt Alix had prolonged her visit; my father was back from Russia; Christmas and New Year's passed by—the two Christmases, the two New Year's. The Roman and the Greek festivals succeeded each other at an interval of thirteen days, repeating four times the torture of hope and the agony of disappointment. None of the family seemed to suspect that I was waiting for a gift I had not received. Mlle. Vignot, however, tried to cure me of my passion, now that she thought my aunt had abandoned the idea of giving me the bird.

"Parrots," she told me, "are famous for their stupidity, and besides, they're really very de-

39

structive. They gnaw everything in reach. . . . Haven't I told you about my godmother in Nantes? She had a parrot that she let out of his cage every day. One morning when he was alone in the room, he ate the beautiful plush hat she only wore on Sundays. Parrots moult every year; they're naked and ugly till the feathers grow back, and they're always tiresome when they talk. Sometimes they die from a nasty wart on their tongues. They repeat the same words over and over again. Their bites are infectious. And they have no real affection for any one in the world."

My dear governess, with whom I was reading the *Fables* of La Fontaine, hoped to convince me by these remarks that my lovely parrot was too green, like the grapes that were out of reach. But I was not a Russian fox, much less a Norman fox, and my heart was too generous to despise anything because it was inaccessible. After she left me, I answered her arguments one by one. Why should I seek for intelligence in a creature that glowed with the genius of life—a creature that glittered, moved, and spoke? My good Vignot had no idea that even if he had eaten all my hats, and all hers besides, my parrot would still have been as dear to me as ever. To reproach him with always repeating the same words impressed me as being vain and foolish. At luncheon, when we ate with my parents, didn't they make the same remarks day after day? Didn't they always repeat, "Ah, if Sasha had only lived!" and "When our angel comes back again"?

As for affection, hadn't my parrot chosen me that famous morning? Let him cling to me, if he liked, with beak and claws! A bite from him would hurt me far less than this gnawing, unsatisfied desire.

❧

My birthday came at last. Henceforth the anniversary of my appearance in the world would coincide with that of my greatest sorrow.

I had spent the preceding night in prayer. I regarded it as a holy vigil, and without letting anybody know, I had managed to eat no supper. My Christian education had quite naturally inspired me to practices from which I expected a miraculous effect. Meanwhile I waited, heartsick with hope.

Mlle. Vignot, having overheard the instructions given by Aunt Alix, had repeated them to me the day before. Henceforth I could abandon myself unhesitatingly to the transports of my desire, as to a rising tide which would cast me tomorrow, shipwrecked and overjoyed, on the shores of Paradise. I saw the sun come up. I crawled into bed only to disarrange the covers and rise again immediately. At the usual time, the maid came to open the curtains, which I had closed only a moment before.

When I went downstairs for breakfast, I saw, through the glass door of the veranda, which opened on the park, the bird-fancier approaching on foot by the little path that wound among the tamarisks, the one we called "the postman's path." At the end of a stick, he carried a cage, in which the green bird was sitting tranquilly. A child followed him like a falconer's page, bearing the perch, the chain, and the cups for food and water. The doors of the house opened wide before the expected guest. A servant hastened to inform Aunt Alix. I was paralyzed with joy; I could not speak or make a movement. I did not dare to go forward. I tried to hide myself behind the glass door, as if ashamed of my happiness and horrified; I was like a young girl who has received an unexpected proposal. The bird-fancier saw me; doubtless he knew my story; he laid down the cage and said:

"Come here, Miss, and stroke his head; he's tame."

With my emotion gripping me like a hand at my throat, I passed my hand through the gilt bars. The bird, which had been hopping up and down in a sort of Spanish dance, began to run along his perch eagerly. He stretched out his neck and put his head to one side, in an attitude of pleased expectancy. At last I dared to run my finger over his little flat head, smoothing his feathers that were as fine as a mown lawn, drawing quite near his fearsome beak. . . .

What happened afterwards took place in the livid glow that precedes a stroke of lightning.

We were still in the hallway: myself, Aunt Alix, and the bird-fancier. I had taken the cage in my hand. A door opened, that of the library, and my father appeared. He took a few steps in our direction, waving his newspaper. His tall body was somewhat stooped; he had let his glasses fall by their ribbon; his eyes were vague, his hair ruffled, his beard in disorder, and he had the flurried look of people who have been interrupted after plunging into their reading as into a sleep full of dreams.

"My dear Alix," he said, "I beg you not to give this parrot to the child; her whim is really absurd."

Ah! I was sinking . . . I was drowning in the sea . . . the water had blinded me, deafened me . . . it was rising and I was falling deeper, deeper; at last it closed over my head, and through its buzzing depths I heard my father drone on, in the same tone of voice:

"Read this story in the *Temps*, my dear Alix— a whole family infected by a tuberculous cockatoo. . . . Why, it caused the death of seventeen people in one house. . . . And the same birds are capable of spreading diphtheria. You can't have forgotten that Sasha died of diphtheria. . . ."

Aunt Alix did not answer; the bird-fancier, too, said nothing . . . nobody spoke the few words that would have saved me.

My father went up to the parrot's owner and indicated by a wave of his hand that the bird should be taken away. The man would be given something for his pains. . . .

He nodded, bent forward, lifted his burden again, and walked down the hall toward the kitchen, carrying the cage in front of him on the stick. My father went back to the library; my aunt followed. The portières swung shut behind them. . . . I was alone. . . . I had nothing, nothing. . . .

45

CHAPTER V

THE DEATH OF DESIRE

ON THE night that preceded my vigil, I had dreamt of being pursued. I was fleeing through a vast, gloomy forest. Men on horseback were galloping after me; I heard the drumming of hoofs. My clothes torn, my hair streaming in the wind, I ran with all my strength toward a last refuge, a glade where a little house stood hidden among very old trees; it had doors that I could barricade.

With one step, I crossed the threshold. I climbed the stairs breathlessly, crossed an empty room, ran toward an open window, and there, feeling that the pursuit would continue, that the horsemen would catch up with me and batter down the doors, that already the wind of their mad gallop was playing in my hair, suddenly I realized that I should rather die than be captured, and deliberately leaped from the window.

What happened on the fatal day when I possessed and lost the green parrot in the same moment, was nothing like the dream. But I had been warned in a vision, as it were, that if placed in extreme circumstances, between the agony of being taken and that of death, I should choose to die. Rather than submit to misfortune, I should find a way of escape.

What were the vague forces within me that produced the dream? Was I not already the unconscious victim of the typhoid fever that was to reveal itself two days later? Accidents are always prepared for; they *exist*, as it were, before taking place; the work of revolution is accomplished before the barricades are built.

As soon as the kitchen door had closed on the bird-fancier, I ran breathlessly up the stairs to the nursery. It was a large room in the upper story, on the side facing the sea; it had been half empty since my sisters went away. I burst into it, still

47

fleeing; I passed through several doors, closing them after me as in my dream, then rushed into my own room and flung open the casement window. Great camellia bushes, almost the size of trees, were coming into bloom beneath me, in the shelter of a projecting ledge. For some vague reason, they prevented me from carrying out my original design. I heard a voice in the linen closet, which was separated from my room by a thin partition. Old Nianka was singing a Russian lullaby:

> *The sun and the moon*
> *Were brother and sister:*
> *Balalaika, balalaika,*
> *Niem the balalaika. . . .*

Was it the fear of crushing the lovely camellias that held me back as I leaned out of the window so far above them? Was it because I heard old Nianka's song?

In my dream, I had jumped from a lower window, but had fallen on the bare ground where I was sure to be killed. I stepped back from the windowsill. In the alcove where my bed was placed, a skipping-rope hung like a votive offering beside my crucifix. I had placed it there after a terrible quarrel with Olga the trouble-maker. It belonged to my older sisters, who had given it to me when they left, but Olga always threatened to take it away. She had really never learned to use it, and disliked exercise of any sort, but because I skipped rope very well, she tried to prevent me. My lightness weighed upon her; my agility exhausted her. Heavy and always complaining, she could not follow me, even with her eyes. Her soul was jaundiced like her complexion; and I still did not dream that I should one day have to forgive the evil she wrought, since it resulted from a sorrow the cause of which was not in herself.

I climbed on a chair to reach the disputed cord, which I had left in the keeping of God to frighten Olga; she still threatened, however, to come into my room and cut it down with a pair of scissors she had stolen. I felt not the least fear, being wholly occupied with another thought. The image of a forgotten event, which had happened more than a year before, was mirrored in my mind with extraordinary clearness.

The previous spring, a man had hanged himself in the grounds of a neighboring villa—Calaouça, it was called. The maids had gone to see him, and notwithstanding the strict injunctions of my parents, they had talked of his death so often, in veiled terms, that we finally learned the whole story. The man who committed suicide was a young postman, whose route had lain through the scattered villas along the shore. We all knew him at the house, for he brought our mail. One April evening, in a fit of drunkenness or melancholy—no one was quite sure of his motive—on his way out of the villa, he had leaned his bicycle against a great tree, behind the wall of the kitchen garden, and climbing to the first large branch, had slipped a noose round his neck. . . . Miss Grey declared that he was neurasthenic, and the maids that he was in love, but though I racked my head, I could understand neither the first term nor the second. Our family physician, when I asked him about it, seemed very angry, and I learned on this occasion that some things are not to be discussed.

On the night of the suicide, no one had felt that anything was wrong. It was not till the following morning that the gardener, on his way to work, had seen the abandoned bicycle, and above it the young postman swaying in the tree. But the Pekingese in the villa of Calaouça had kept their mistress awake all night with their barking, as if they suspected. . . .

With the same dreamlike movements as before, I had run out of my room, carrying the rope. Old Nianka, when she saw me passing the door to the linen closet, which was always open as a trap for children, called out to me:

"Where are you going in such a hurry, my dove?"

"To the garden, Nianka, to skip rope!"

I went to the corner of the park where my mother's hammock was hung in the summer. A giant pine stood there, with its straight branches symmetrically spaced. In the days when I had visions, I thought of it as a sort of Jacob's ladder standing against the sky, so that Sasha could climb down with the angels.

I was going to use this prophetic tree as a means of leaving the earth. The cord felt cool to my neck. I was still perspiring after my long run.

*

It was Mlle. Vignot who found me and cut me down. She carried me away in her arms, though even when I was nine, my body was long and heavy. But horror had given her new strength.

When I recovered consciousness, I burst into a great flood of tears. I can remember nothing more. They put me to bed; I was delirious when the doctor came; he declared that I was threatened with typhoid fever, that the disease had probably been developing for some time, and that my excitement of the morning and the preceding days was only a symptom.

My illness lasted for several weeks, during which I was left in profound isolation. The mother of a numerous family must abandon all thoughts of nursing the child who suffers from a contagious disease. Yet I had often heard that my parents spent night and day with Sasha during his last illness. On that occasion it was the healthy members of the family who were avoided for fear of contagion. . . . Mlle. Vignot alone watched over me, with a devotion that was all the more admirable because she was young, a new arrival in the house, and because she owed us nothing.

As soon as I was strong enough to travel, I was sent to visit some relatives of ours, who were Russians of Cannes. There, for the first time, I found that I was liked. I met the man who was to marry me six years later. He was almost thirty, and I was not yet ten. His parents were mourning a daughter of my own age, and for her sake they watched over me and caressed me as my own family had never done.

When I returned to Biarritz, I had grown much taller and seemed more robust than before. My hair had been cut short during my illness, and since then it had grown abundantly. Everybody remarked that my appearance was much improved. The moral change was even greater. I had become indifferent; I had become gay. Just as my organism had killed the germs of typhoid, I had killed in myself the germs of all desire. I had sworn to wish for nothing, and in fact, I felt myself totally incapable of desiring anything whatsoever.

"It is a disease that never comes back," our old physician told my mother. "Your daughter will be immune for the rest of her days."

PART TWO

SISTER MARIE

CHAPTER VI

THE SOLITUDE OF ANGLET

IN GENERAL the people of Biarritz have a to-pographical knowledge that extends from the Côte des Basques to Port-Vieux, from the Rock of the Virgin to the Place Ste. Eugénie, and from the Casino to the Grande Plage. When it comes to excursions, their knowledge of itineraries is more extensive, and reaches from Hendaye to St. Jean-de-Luz, from Bayonne to the Bar of the Adour, from Cambo into Spain; but I doubt that one in a hundred could tell you the road to the Solitude of Anglet.

I could recognize it with my eyes closed, if asked to choose from all the roads of the world. No other has the same curious power of deadening one's footsteps. During my childhood, when I walked there with my mother, it seemed to me that the fine white sand might be transformed at any moment into a quicksand, and that deaf to all the cries of the world, I should be engulfed in its profound silence.

To reach this muted pathway, one drives through a forest of maritime pines, where other roads branch off at frequent intervals. An arrow on the left points toward the "Chamber of Love," and most of the carriages strike off in this direction. My mother and I would turn to the right instead, along a driveway bordered with low dikes that were covered with yuccas. When these plants were in bloom, I was almost afraid to look at them, they were so tall and white, so much like ghosts stalking through the twilight of the woods. I called them "lilies-of-the-valley for giants."

We always climbed out of the carriage on reaching the avenue of silence. Across the roadway is a wooden fence, placed there as a bar to vehicles. Only pedestrians are admitted to the road that kills all sounds; it is trodden only by human feet. A wooden signboard standing midway in the path requests all visitors to speak in a low voice. The injunction is useless, for you are reveling already in the charms of a silence you have no wish to break.

Nothing guards the Solitude of Anglet except the solitude itself; there is neither a gatekeeper's lodge nor a sister standing watch; no bell announces the arrival of intruders; there is no bolt, no lock; and, if you have the courage, you need merely open a wooden gate that swings noiselessly on well-oiled hinges.

On the left you pass a low building that is hidden, except for its roof, by a carefully tended hedge of camellias. When the hedge is in blossom, the scene is enchanting, for all the flowers are red. Shortly afterwards, it is even more lovely; the petals fall abundantly before fading, and for days they preserve the coolness and brilliance of polished marble. You are entering a path of porphyry.

Two nuns in black, who do not belong to the order of the Bernardines, live in a little hut that guards the entrance to the inner Solitude. They greet the visitors, and while one of them hastens to warn the Solitaries that the holy calm is being desecrated, the other acts as your guide through this Thebaid. Always she opens one of the tiny cells, calls your attention to its perfect bareness, points to a wooden box in the corner that serves as a bed, strikes it with her knuckles till it echoes like a coffin, then says for the edification of the world:

"This cell is inhabited."

Afterwards she takes you to the refectory, a long, floorless hut built on the bare sand and lighted by tiny unglazed windows. The table of deal boards is low and narrow. Each separate place is set with a bowl, a wooden spoon, and a water jug. There are neither chairs nor benches, for the Bernardines take their meals standing.

"They eat on their knees every Friday," says the sister, bent on expounding the rule that is observed by every one in the Solitude except herself and her companion. She is like an ant explaining the home-life of bees to a group of strangers. She next leads you to a low wooden building where once a year these voluntary mutes break their

vows of silence and speak with their nearest relatives; then to the miraculous chapel where they
offer up their prayers, which must be neither
chanted nor spoken, but secretly distilled like
honey in a flower; then to the garden, where day
after day, with a ditch-digger's shovel in their
hands, they cultivate their graves.

At the age of nine, thanks to my mother, I began to frequent the Solitude of Anglet. We came
there so often that the two black-robed sisters let
us wander alone, being certain that we should
never disturb the silence. If, at a bend in the
path, we passed a sort of woolen bag surmounted
with a gardener's hat, we knew that it was a Bernardine; we said nothing, and did not even stare
at the face that was hidden beneath the straw
brim. We were not tourists full of indiscreet curiosity, but real friends of St. Bernard and an-
chorites ourselves. . . .

On my return from Cannes after my conva-
lescence, our visits became more frequent. Sup-
posedly my mother was taking me to the Solitude in order to thank the Virgin for saving my

life. As a matter of fact, her pilgrimage was one of supplication, not of thanksgiving, and I was supposed to join my innocent prayers to hers. We visited the little chapel every week, at an hour agreed upon with the black-robed sister, and there prayed before the curious Spanish madonna that so resembled the Empress Eugénie.

The chapel was a straw hut with a thatched roof; it resembled the primitive beehives which can still be seen in a few Basque gardens. Like all the buildings in the Solitude, it was built directly on the sand, without a foundation. The ceiling was so low that a tall person could have touched it by lifting his arms toward Heaven. When we prayed there, our knees left two round holes in the sand, which had to be smoothed out after we had risen. An inscription to the right of the door attested that in this chapel, Emperor Napoleon III and Empress Eugénie had implored Our Lady of Solitude to send them a son; their prayers were answered in 1856, when the Prince Imperial was born.

Underneath this plaque were listed the names of other illustrious visitors who had worshiped in this holy hut: Victoria, Queen of Great Britain, and Ireland; Frederica, Princess of Hanover; the Prince of Wales; the Prussian princes; the grand dukes of Hesse and of Russia; the King of Spain. . . .

I liked to repeat these names, which evoked unknown places, floras, and climates. Almost all of the thoughts they suggested to my mind were connected with the vegetable kingdom. Victoria was a giant water-lily of Lake Tchad, in which a child could sit, riding the waves; Hanover, for some vague reason, represented a hemp-blossom; Prussia was a Prussian-blue cornflower; Wales—Galles in French—was an oak-gall, from which one could make ink; the grand dukes were horned owls, and like everything in Russia they smelt of tanned leather and violets; finally I pictured the King of Spain as a pomegranate blossom, red as coral and lovely as a jewel; he was a flower like the one I had been given by an old

Spanish peddlar as I came from vespers one evening—for love, so he said, of my long yellow hair. Each of these names suggested a little poem, which I afterwards recited in a low voice. I had plenty of time for these floral games, the curious rules of which were determined by myself alone; for, when I knelt in the chapel once a week beside my mother, I did not pray; I merely pretended to pray.

To desire something—to implore Heaven for any gift whatever—impressed me as being a shameful weakness, of which, for my part, I was forever cured. I had prayed for something ardently, and not having obtained it, I had nearly been killed by the disappointment. The Empress, too, had prayed; she had fallen on her knees before the same image of the Virgin to which my mother was now addressing her vows; she had even been granted the boon she asked— and to what avail? Her son, the object of all her prayers, had died in exile from a poisoned arrow, and this loss was worse than the mere absence of joy; it was a sorrow inherent in the joy that preceded it, a sorrow that rendered the granted prayer both vain and ridiculous.

Why insist on wishing, when even after obtaining what you wish, you are liable to lose it? Your good fortune will be merely another opportunity for fate to betray you. As I knelt beside my mother, who was obstinately beseeching the Virgin to bring back Sasha, now that she was expecting another child, I refrained from adding my prayers to hers. I remarked on the fiery heat that reigned in the chapel, where the air under the low roof was parched by the sand; I slipped out; I asked if I could finish telling my beads in the garden. As a matter of fact, I had not even begun; I skipped through the verses; my rosary had become a mere device by which to remember little poems of my own.

I opened a little door at the end of the garden and entered the graveyard of the Bernardines. Strange as it may seem, this was the spot in all the world where I was happiest. I had a sense of delicious calm; I felt myself sheltered from everything; I had found peace and deliverance.

The graveyard was a little desert surrounded by a paling and bisected by an alley of cypress trees, down which I strolled. To my right and left were rows of symmetrical dunes the size of a recumbent body: it almost seemed that the Bernardines had played at making sand-pies, employing a coffin for a mold instead of a tin pail. Then, on the hastily smoothed surface of these mounds, they had made a cross of white shells. A fan-shaped wave would soon creep upwards from the sea, and these little houses of sand would disappear in a moment.

I have seen in later days the famous cemeteries of Constantinople and the Towers of Silence erected by the Zoroastrians in the deserts of Asia. They gave me no such impression of equality in death as I felt among the graves of the Bernardines, which were built of sand in the sand, and seemed so fragile that a child with his bare hands, in a very few minutes, could have destroyed every trace of them forever.

To this place of rest prepared for themselves by

women solely concerned with disappearing, I came once a week to learn a lesson of indifference which I was destined to remember all my life. My mother, meanwhile, was in the little chapel, once more beseeching Heaven to restore the son who had first been given her, then taken away. She seemed to think that by a mysterious law of balance, a necessary compensation, this Virgin adored by persons who had renounced everything, would show herself particularly attentive to the prayers of those who wished violently to obtain a definite boon.

One day, when my soul was soothed by the delicious perfume of silence that filled the Solitude, I said to my mother:

"Oh, wouldn't I like to be a Bernardine!"

Taking me at my word, and believing that I had found my vocation, she pressed me to her bosom—a gesture so unexpected that it caused me more fright than pleasure.

If she could promise her daughter along with her other vows; if she could offer me up as a ho-

locaust, make a gift of me to the Virgin of Anglet, what might she not expect as a recompense
for this sacrifice?

And we returned to the house by the alley of
yuccas, my mother feeling that I had offered myself as a ransom for my brother, and I knowing
that I had freed myself from her bondage completely and forever.

CHAPTER VII

MARIE

MARIE came into the world when I was ten years old, and my life was already over when hers began.

That a child of my age, who had been restored to physical vigor after an unexpected illness, should be too deeply injured ever to recover her emotional health, seems almost impossible to imagine. Yet this was the moral accident I had suffered. It had caused me, so I felt, to lose the faculty of hope, just as another accident might have deprived me of the faculties of sight or hearing.

Nineteen years later, Marie would write me:

"You have everything, and wish for nothing whatsoever."

In the year of her birth, it was true already that I had ceased to wish for anything, that I

had renounced my will, that I lived without desires—which is almost the same as not living.
This state of resignation, when combined with
the advantages of beauty and social position,
was destined to assure me a life full of little
triumphs—though, as I neither anticipated nor
took advantage of them, they left me so indifferent and detached that I wondered how I could
ever grow old, having found nothing to mark the
years as they passed.

A few days before Marie was born, we were
sent away from the house, so that our presence
should not frighten off the angel who surely, this
time, was bringing back our brother. By listening to old Nianka's monologues, from which I
had learned that Sasha, instead of having flown
away, was really dead "like everybody else," I
now heard that the doctor was to sleep in my
room and the nurse in that of my sisters.

We spent a week at Calaouça, near Lake Marion, with the Russian lady who knew our parents. One clear winter morning, my father came

70

to take us home. Watching his dark carriage as it rolled along the road in the sunlight, under the leafless trees, we wondered what news he was bringing. He saw us waiting at the bend in the driveway and waved his hand. The gesture seemed dispirited; I felt that his tidings were evil. For the third and last time, Heaven had said, No!

"Children, you have a little sister," my father announced. "Her name will be Marie."

I accepted Marie, and I was the only one in all our household to do so. My mother wept helplessly, and refused to see the child who had put an end to her hopes. The disappointment extended from large to small, from my father to the least of our servants. Old Nianka wailed that we should never again see Russia, and she cursed the Pope, "the woman of Lourdes," the Holy Virgin of the Catholics, and the day when she herself was born.

My mother was already more than forty; every one in the family realized that we should have to abandon the idea of bringing Sasha back to the world. It was through Marie that the harsh refusal of Heaven was definitely announced.

The layette had been trimmed with lovely blue ribbons, in expectation of the son that Marie was not. The nurse took them out, under orders; she replaced them with our old pink ribbons. Nobody looked at the new baby. Her airings were a secret matter: she was taken out by the servants' door, and wheeled along paths that were hidden from the eyes of her grieving mother. Though the newcomer had been so poorly received, Olga the trouble-maker was jealous, and gave her the nickname of "Mademoiselle de Trop." I alone, in this disappointed family, had learned to wish for nothing, to expect nothing, and the fortunate effects of my detachment were visible already. I did not fall into the error of the others: they were angry at innocent Marie for being a girl, and therefore treated her as a culprit. My conscience was not burdened with this iniquity.

*

I sometimes went to see her in her crib, which once had been my own. Furtively I kissed her blind little forehead and looked with pitying curiosity at her tiny hands, lost and trembling, that opened and closed like starfish in the void.

CHAPTER VIII

SISTER AND SISTER

A WOMAN of the eighteenth century, a very witty woman who lacked a male heir, said to her friends:

"I have always had a son in my head, but I could never give birth to him."

After Marie was born, my mother might have repeated these words. It was in vain that my parents had mentally conceived the double of their son; physical conception had followed another course, and in their last child they beheld my double instead. Marie was a replica of myself, something that no one had been expecting. She so resembled me that her first photographs might have been taken for mine. Of course, after she passed the age when babies are made to pose in long white dresses, our pictures could be dis-

tinguished from each other, if only by the different cut of our frocks.

The Circassian blood that unites southern
Russia to Persia was manifested in one of my sisters by the way her heavy eyebrows joined together, and in another by the blackness of her
curly hair. All of them were dark except Marie,
who was as blonde and rosy as myself. It seemed
that the two of us had issued from another line,
that we were marked with a northern heredity,
that in us the icy current of the Gulf of Finland
had made its way to the heart of the southern re-
gions from which our parents had come; we were
their boreal daughters.

A face that has been eclipsed for five or six generations returns like a star to the human horizon.
When the star of Marie, rising from what infi-
nite depths of night I could not say, dawned over
me one morning, I thought I was reliving my
own childhood. She was a mirror that revealed
the changing image of my past. At fifteen, I saw
myself as I had been at five; at twenty, I beheld

the little girl I was at ten. Marie inherited my dead self; she had my hair and eyes; she had also my room, my textbooks, and the friendship of my dear Vignot.

*

When I married, I was forced to renounce the world of my childhood. This is the common lot of young women, and it is in this respect above all others that marriage is like taking the veil. I pronounced my vows early, at sixteen, in fact, and not having been allowed to finish my childhood, I regarded it with the mixture of regret and longing that is the aftermath of interrupted pleasures.

When the eldest son of our relatives at Cannes asked for my hand, I accepted his proposal without hesitation. I had known Andrei ever since my illness, and this impressed me as being a great advantage. I was terrified by the fate of my elder sisters: they had married men of whom they knew nothing, not even their family names, three months before taking these names for themselves.

Our unequal union was soon consummated. To my father it seemed quite advantageous. He regarded the great difference in age between Andrei and myself as the only serious obstacle, and hence he was in great haste to remove it.

"If we wait six months more," he said, "you will be hardly less young, whereas your husband will be a whole year older."

The first time my marriage was discussed in a family council, my father had insisted on the fact that my uncle of Cannes was only an uncle by marriage, and that Andrei Mikhailovitch, being the son of his first wife, was in no respect my cousin. It would almost have seemed that the absence of relationship was, to my father, a stronger argument in favor of this suitor than was his birth, his health, or his considerable fortune.

The wedding took place in St. Martin's, the old parish church, one day in February. On the way to the ceremony, I passed the little moss-grown path I had taken with my mother on the famous morning when I fell in love with the green parrot. Seeing primroses and daisies along the hedgerows, I remembered the emotion I once felt at the sight of these flowers. At present I felt no emotion whatsoever, though all my future was being decided.

Marie was waiting for me on the steps of the old church. She was to carry my train, and, as she was only six and the train very heavy, I could feel, as I advanced toward the altar, her little hands clutching the white silk and holding me back.

❧

When we first established ourselves in Cannes, I felt more exiled on the Mediterranean than if I had changed, not coasts, but countries and even continents. And three years after my marriage, when I received my husband's permission to return to the Gulf of Gascony and to spend a week out of every year in my father's house, it seemed to me that I was making a much longer journey through time than the simple trip from Nice to Bordeaux and from Bordeaux to Bayonne that I accomplished on the map. I returned to my former universe and did not find it empty. My place was taken: I survived in Marie. Was it she I loved, or merely my own shadow? I softly opened the door of the schoolroom; a blonde head was bending over the books Mlle. Vignot had purchased at the Librairie Benquet when I was her pupil and needed an excuse to pass the bird-shop in the Rue Mazagran, where the green parrot, chained to his perch, held my heart in his claws like a sunflower seed. Mlle. Vignot, on whose face the invisible years of my childhood had left no mark, was repeating the same dictation, "Springtime in Brittany," from Chateaubriand. On the margins of my former schoolbooks, which I had covered with little ink-sketches and puns, I read the nicknames I had given them: the Roman history was called Crassus, because its cover was crassly dirty; the arithmetic was surnamed Ragusa, and was really falling into rags from having been too often mishandled by a stormy little girl who had no bump of mathematics. Marie raised her head; she smiled at me before she embraced me. She admired in me the young woman that she would

79

soon become; I loved in her the child I had ceased
to be. Both of us troubled, one by memories, the
other by hopes, we could not look at each other
without emotion; I was her future; she was my
living past.

Our resemblance, which was universally remarked, made us very fond of each other. My sister was an integral part of my self-love. In everything that concerned her, I obeyed the divine
commandment without difficulty: truly I loved
her as myself. If this degree of perfection in love
is rarely attained, is it not the fault of our neigh-
bor, who always resembles us so little? Marie
found favor in my eyes, and I in hers. As each of
us looked at the other's face, we felt all the pleasures of self-content and none of its shame. If
some one saw me staring at myself in a mirror,
doubtless I should turn away my eyes. I admired
the innocent beauty of Marie with no feeling
of guilt. I spoke of her without reticence, without suffering the pangs of false modesty or
the blushes of embarrassment. It was by study-
ing the girlish face of my younger sister that I

learned to read the omens of the mysterious triumph of nature for which I had been merely a sort of preliminary sketch.

I have always been amused by one expression of my English friends. They say of a beautiful woman, "She has looks," and of a woman who has ceased to be beautiful, "Her looks are gone." Marie *had looks* as soon as she appeared. However, it was not till her fifteenth year that she taught me what this particular quality is in itself. I was trying to find her in the crowd that had gathered on the Bridge of the Virgin, one evening when the equinoctial tide was rising, to see the shipwreck of the sun. Already the vessel of fire was plunging into the sea, and Mlle. Vignot had not yet appeared with my sister. As I waited, leaning against the parapet of the bridge, I looked at the faces about me, all of them pitilessly revealed by the stormy rays of a half-submerged sun.

There, when I saw Marie approaching among the other women, I understood that beauty is not "a promise of happiness." It is an instant of realized happiness, something resembling the happy ending of a little mathematical drama. I had been trying to make a rapid calculation on each face that passed by: would the addition of the traits distributed on the surface of the face give me the exact sum of pleasure I was expecting? Each time, the calculation proved incorrect; I felt the twinge of embarrassment and displeasure that follows a mistake in arithmetic. All these women were ugly. Suddenly Marie appeared, and I felt with a glow of satisfaction that I had found the correct answer. Eureka! I breathed more freely. When I began my problem in addition, I had been hoping to arrive at this sum. Obviously those about us had found the same solution. All of them turned to stare at Marie; all seemed happy at having seen the miracle; they wished to verify the magic figure and fix it in their memories. When she appeared, each one agreed with himself and with all the others. Her passage through the crowd left a long wake of contentment.

This first effect of beauty is the only one that

is not mixed with bitterness; it puts men in unison and makes them understand one another. Later they begin to quarrel over the ownership of this treasure, which at first was held in common. The charm is broken immediately; what had caused agreement becomes a reason for dispute; what had pleased is now a source of unhappiness; and in this second phase, which follows all too soon after the first, Marie would have to pay dearly for the joy she thought to give. When this time comes, the girl with "looks" should, if she loves peace, hasten to disappear from the eyes of the world. The same quality that made her loved will cause her to be hated; wherever she goes, women will arm themselves against her, and the men, who always end by adopting women's judgments, will be enrolled among her enemies. He who marries her, ceasing to be astonished by her beauty, will soon cease to behold it; faced with a daily miracle, he will no longer have the strength to believe in miracles. He possesses the magic ring that renders his wife invisible; soon he will see nothing but other women. A few years after their marriage, no trace of his love will remain—not even jealousy, its skeleton. As a mere observer of emotions he no longer shares, the husband will see men aspiring toward his wife, competing for her favors, and he will be unable to understand their madness. The passion that animates them will seem ridiculous to him, like the movements of dancers to a deaf man. Just so long as the woman who "has looks" repulses her suitors, every other woman will feel herself to be threatened; one always fears the lightning till it has struck. And if she has the weakness to choose a lover, then, to the legitimate hate of the woman from whom she has taken him—for there is no such thing on earth as a free man—will be added the uneasy hate of other women—for how can they believe that she will not change?—and the declared hate of the men, all of whom will feel themselves injured. And who will console the grieving heart of the woman who "has looks"?

I began to regard my sister's features as those of a young martyr about to be thrown to the beasts. Of the harpies who would soon assemble to tear her to pieces, not one would have the wit to say, "What is the use of all these efforts? Is she not destined for the deepest shame? Let time work for us. It will condemn her to ignominy and death. One by one it will obliterate the marks of her power; it will degrade her before the eyes of the world; we shall be present at her fall; those who have known her will recognize her no longer; and even before she is forgotten, she will become a stranger to herself."

I saw the Empress Eugénie at the age of ninety-two; like Marie Antoinette, whose fate she once feared, she had lost her head; it had been replaced by another; instead of the charming features that so resembled those of the Virgin of Anglet, she had the face of an old crone. In this poor degraded creature . . . I found only one trace of the sovereign woman: the pure line of her nose. I attached my eyes with respect to the little that remained of her celebrated charms, now almost completely dissolved by time. Just as a single column standing among the ruins is enough to give the dimensions of a Greek temple, so the nose of the Empress Eugénie had enabled me to reconstruct the image of her vanished beauty.

That day on the Bridge of the Virgin, when my sister Marie came toward me looking so different from other mortals, I said to myself: "May she always be satisfied with this pleasure as light as the breath of the wind, this joy of seeing men bow down like the grass as she sweeps by, and may she put her trust only in the blind love of the poor governess who has taught her all she knows!"

CHAPTER IX

LORD MANFRED OF GATCHINA

AT THE time of my marriage, I had never been in Russia, and it was several years before my husband took me there for the first time. He himself was almost totally ignorant of his native country. Living in Cannes with his family, he had only one occupation, polo, and only one fatherland, the polo fields of the world. This fatherland changed with the seasons. We spent the winter in Cannes, the spring in Madrid, the early summer in Roehampton, the late summer in Deauville.

One year we even went to India, where we found the same clipped greensward, the same white stakes, the same riders on their little horses, and the sound of the same bell. My husband once told me, shortly after our marriage:

"I rather feel that I shall want to be hitting

87

some one all my life. So I hit a ball instead, and sometimes I give it a name."

Ten years later I saw him hitting away with all his might, but it never entered my head to ask him what name he was giving the ball.

As I lived among the Centaurs and always traveled with a stable, I came to take a lively interest in horses, my companions. They were the only living creatures that caused me no pain, and hence I preferred their society to that of men. Polo ponies are really delightful: their legs are delicately articulated, like the stems of carnations; they have quivering nostrils, proud eyes, animated features; and if you observe them closely in the course of a hardfought game, you will see that their intelligence is almost as keen as that of their masters, and sometimes far keener: they take part in the game, and in more than one difficult situation, I have noticed that the horse made up his mind before the rider.

In 1914, my husband was invited to Russia; he was to found a polo club in the suburbs of St. Petersburg. He decided to sacrifice his annual trip to Spain, and that spring we embarked for Reval with the ponies.

On this occasion I became acquainted with Russia and with all my relatives. It seemed to me that I was adopting a second country, since I still regarded Biarritz as my native soil.

The doors to the paradise of Gatchina were opened for me; I could enter without fear. The grandfather who had driven out my parents was no longer of this world. At present my father was living in voluntary exile from an estate which had become his by right of inheritance.

When, among the trees with their branches twisted by the snows of too many winters, I first perceived the "Gatchina Gatchinushka" that old Nianka had celebrated so often and mourned so bitterly, I realized that our villa in Biarritz, with its Italianate roof, its pilasters, and its First Empire look, was only a copy of this old Russian house. My parents had tried to reproduce, at the other end of Europe, the world they possessed in their childhood and lost by their own sin.

Two aged ladies, vibrant with emotion, were

waiting under a peristyle that I recognized without ever having seen. They were my aunt and my grandmother.

Every family that has preserved the portraits of its members delights in the game of resemblances. After whist, it is the favorite sport of old people. Russia is a country of snuff-boxes, and hence it is also a country of miniatures. From the reign of Catherine II till that of Alexander III, no one in our family had failed to have himself painted on a box.

When I appeared at Gatchina, the first question my aunt asked my grandmother was, "Whom does she take after?"

Then, turning to me:

"Should you say that you take after me, or after your grandmother?"

After a first appraising glance at their two types of ugliness, which were dissimilar on the surface, but equal in depth, I was tempted to reply:

"After neither one nor the other, I should hope!"

What I actually said was, "Really, Aunt Sophie, you must decide for yourself. But they have always told me that except for her beauty, I was the very picture of my sister Marie."

"Nonsense!" exclaimed my aunt, who of course had never seen Marie.

She continued, emphasizing each separate word:

"You are the perfect image of Maria Serguyevna Dalgorukin, your great-grandmother, a very great beauty who was called the Rose of St. Petersburg."

And to prove her point, she opened the cabinet where the snuff-boxes were kept, and took out a tortoise-shell box made at the beginning of the nineteenth century. Inside the cover, in a circle of gold, was the portrait of a very young woman whose blonde hair and fresh tint I had certainly inherited. I also recognized, on her smiling mouth, the delicate expression that gave Marie's lips a sort of perpetual laughter, while the slanting line of her eyelids seemed sad by comparison.

At the bottom of the box was a thin tortoise-shell disc that could be removed completely and slid into a second exterior groove, thus revealing the portrait of a young man placed in a golden circle similar to the first.

Two unknown names were engraved in a half-moon on the metal ring: APHERIDON—ASTARTE. The inside of the cover bore a motto arranged as a rebus:

(*J'ai la clef du cœur*—I have the key of the heart.)

When the box was open, the two pictures faced each other, but once it was closed, they lay one above the other in the darkness.

The young woman's face and that of the young man did not resemble each other in the least, and this led me to believe that I was looking at the portraits of the Rose of St. Petersburg and her husband.

92

But my grandmother disabused me. The two miniatures contained in the oval box were those of Maria Dalgorukin and her brother Alexander. He wore a white uniform; his hair had the disheveled look that was cultivated by the dandies of his era; his deep brown eyes slanted upwards; he had a dark, imperfect sort of beauty that was calculated to impress itself on women's memories. In so far as the face of a young officer who took part in the Battle of Waterloo can resemble that of a little boy who was born seventy years later, I found in this miniature of 1816 a great family likeness to the portraits of Sasha.

I was not unduly surprised at this resemblance: unlike ordinary families, we had only a single line of descent. Through my mother and my father, we went back to the same source, that of Maria Serguyevna, and consequently to that of her brother Alexander. Had not old Nianka taught us in our childhood to mourn this anomaly, which she called "the great sin"? It was, she believed, the cause of all our misfortunes, beginning with the death of Sasha.

93

Vainly Mlle. Vignot had tried to destroy my feeling of predestination, which she claimed was un-Christian. "We are all descended from Adam," she told me, to counteract the effect of the nurse's words, which were troubling my young mind. But she did not succeed in destroying my fear of the mysterious flaw existing within us. My sister shared my anxiety, as I one day realized from a remark of hers that frightened me by its implications.

Mounet-Sully was playing in Bayonne. With my parents' permission I had taken Marie, who was ten years old at the time, to see a performance of *Oedipus Tyrannus*.

"But why shouldn't he have gone blind after marrying his mother?" she said as we were leaving the theater. "After all, it's bad enough just to marry one's first cousin."

&

A family vault is a sort of museum where the dead of one generation after another are dated, named, catalogued, and laid side by side on shelves.

At Gatchina, in the depths of the vast park, behind a curtain of aged fir-trees with long silver beards on their dry branches, is a chapel standing above a crypt. Younger firs have been planted in great numbers round the chapel, so as to hide it when the old trees are dead. It is only proper that this building should be so concealed—for, like the water-tank, a disgraceful iron donjon; like the kitchen garden and like the tennis court, an abscess of clay in its wire netting—a mausoleum on the country estate of a respectable family is often quite useful, but never agreeable.

On the second day of my visit, my grandmother asked Aunt Sophie to take me to the vault for a sort of presentation to the dead. I stood in the crypt, between its gleaming walls of white marble, and learned to know our genealogical tree by its roots.

"Here," said my aunt in a drill-master's voice that echoed under the arched roof, "is your great-great-grandfather, Ivan Pavlovitch. With the other conspirators, he entered the bedchamber of the Emperor Paul I, and the Emperor did not leave the room alive. Ivan Pavlovitch was the first of our family to spend his life on his estate. Alexander I, as you can readily see, found it difficult to receive his father's assassin in St. Petersburg. . . . But sometimes he visited Gatchina, to see your great-great-grandfather in his retreat. . . ."

The assassin. . . . So my great-great-grandfather was an assassin? I knew that I should call him "the great patriot."

Was it the result of my French education? As a Russian of Biarritz, everything I had seen since reaching Gatchina had astonished and shocked me; I was a stranger among the Russians of Russia. Above all, I was horrified by their way of neglecting the finer shades of meaning and of calling everything by its proper name.

"Here is your great-grandfather, my father's father," said Aunt Sophie, continuing her obituaries. "His name was Paul Ivanovitch, and he died insane. He was a godson of the Emperor Paul, as his name indicates; here is his daughter,

Anna Pavlovna, who died of love for a rich merchant. Here are the two children of her first marriage, they both died at an early age."

Narrower plaques of marble covered the coffins of the children. Those above the adults were broader, and the slabs that concealed the remains of high imperial dignitaries seemed proportionate to the length of their titles, which were engraved on them in letters of gold. I read there, preceded by the word "victory," the names of battles I had always regarded as defeats. I realized that history has two sides, like a coin, and that each nation has its own point of view. Having learned that the good side was the French side, nothing could make me change my mind; I belonged to Mlle. Vignot's party and should never desert her cause. Waterloo to me would always be the name of a disaster and a "sad plain." I had learned too late that my great-great-grandfather, his brothers, and his sons had given their blood to make the joyous name of Austerlitz the sad name of a Russian defeat.

97

Aunt Sophie, striking the floor with her umbrella, proceeded with her jovial explanations before the tombs of her ancestors.

"Andrei Alexandrovitch, died insane." With the other hand, she crossed herself. "Katerina Ivanovna, who let herself die of hunger after her husband had been killed by her father. . . . A hunting accident," she added quickly, as if to reassure me.

"Anna Ivanovna, died without issue."

In a family as prolific as ours, the sterility of a woman was noted on her tombstone. And would this be written on my tomb also: Died without issue?

The generations overlapped, and descendants preceded their ancestors. A little girl had entered the tomb thirty years before her grandmother. An uncle of nineteen was sleeping his last sleep beside his niece, aged eighty-four. After pacifying the Caucasus, one member of our family had been killed by his rebellious serfs. His son had turned liberal, and had spent much of his life in prison for this crime. A young man had been killed in a duel because he advocated the liberty of the press.

A slab of black marble covered the coffin in which lay the bones of the woman I took after: Maria Serguyevna, the Rose of St. Petersburg. In the eternal night, the brother and sister no longer faced each other, as in the snuff-box; their coffins stood one above the other on different shelves.

"He died long before she did; he was only twenty-four," said my aunt, "a mere boy."

She added:

"Russia lost by his death, for undoubtedly he possessed a true poetic genius. He was also a soldier, and served in France under Alexander I and the Duke of Wellington. At that time, the brother and sister conducted a long correspondence under the names of Apheridon and Astarte, which they had adopted Lord knows why. I shall read you their letters tomorrow. The young people had to be separated to avoid a scandal; they were so much in love that they didn't realize they were committing a crime. Their par-

ents took it upon themselves to give this innocent Lucretia a husband older than herself. She
left the house on the day of her wedding, and
then spent five years on your great-grandfather's
estate in the Crimea. She didn't know that her
brother was dead. The parents had made her
swear not to write him; in their letters they spoke
of Alexander as if he were still living. And it
turned out afterwards that this deception had
been absolutely necessary.

"When Maria Serguyevna learned from a
stranger, whom she met by chance, that her
brother was no longer in this world, she had an
attack of insanity, which was only the first of a
series from which she suffered during the rest of
her life. The attacks affected neither her beauty
nor her intelligence; they recurred at regular intervals. She had borne a child before the first of
them, and later had four other children. This
strange disease is called manic-depressive insanity or *folie circulaire*. It was an isolated case in our
family; no other has ever been known. She died
at an advanced age without having recovered.

She was only nineteen at the time of her marriage, and twenty-four when she learned that her beloved brother was dead.

"Alexander had fastened his gun to a tree and killed himself. It happened in a place called the Belvedere, at the top of this little hill. Standing there, one could formerly see the bend in the driveway beyond the wooden bridge, and watch the carriages that brought visitors to Gatchina or took them away.

"That night he watched the lanterns of the coach in which the bride and groom were riding. The torches of their retinue disappeared into the darkness. Nobody heard the shot. A hedge of fir-trees was planted the following year, and their thick branches now conceal the road by which the daughters of the house drive off with their husbands. . . ."

❧

Next day I read the versified letters they exchanged. A pious hand had transcribed them on the engarlanded pages of an old album. Just before joining his regiment, which was marching off to France for the campaign of 1814, Alexander had sent his sister an epistle in romantic and rather pedestrian verse; it ended with these lines:

> *I will deliver thee or die before thee,*
> *Astarte, having said that I adore thee,*
> *Contented let me die.*

How did the fatal influence of Byron reach Gatchina and find two victims there in the year 1814? Was this seed of madness carried by the wind like the winged seeds of maples or the pollen of certain flowers? Or did some zealous agent spread the spirit of destruction?

Aunt Sophie accused the young English tutor who had been brought to Russia to complete Alexander's education. Was it not rather the very atmosphere that was breathed by these two children? Are there not fashions in feeling just as there are fashions in clothes, and do we not adopt the modes of our own time almost unconsciously?

When Chateaubriand's *René*, apostrophizing

the storms of the heart, gave his *Sylph* the features of a sister he loved too well, a fiery wind went raging across Europe, leaving thousands of young victims in its path. And yet, it is possible that the poet's genius was only expressing a mode of feeling that was imposed on himself, even while he seemed to be imposing it upon others. At the beginning of the nineteenth century, this plague was in the air: Chateaubriand bewailed his forbidden love in phrases incomparably melodious, and the secret of Manfred's sorrows was none other than that which caused the death of René's Sylph.

But why assign a date to the guilty passion of brother for sister and sister for brother? This love kindled in those of the same blood—a blood that seeks after and prefers itself, that finds gratification in itself alone—does it belong to one era rather than another?

Aunt Sophie, as she initiated me into the mystery of Gatchina, seemed bent on making me pity the Rose, my poor great-grandmother. She tried to find excuses for the lovers, and cultivated a romantic veneration for the memory of the handsome Alexander. In her eagerness to win my sympathy for them, in her desire to prove that this sort of curse had existed since the beginning of the world, she even told me a very ancient Russian legend—perhaps it belongs to the cycle of solar myths that are common to all mankind—in which the Slavic Apollo and Diana, brother and sister as in the Greek fable, are represented as victims of the forbidden love:

"The sun and the moon, it is said, loved each other with a guilty love and with mutual desire. And one night in their father's house, the brother stole to the sister's couch and possessed her in secret.

"At the climax of their passion, they were surprised by their mother. She separated them with threats and imprecations. The father drove them out ignominiously and condemned them never to meet again.

"Since that time, the moon rises in the sky only when the sun is sinking. They pursue each other day after day, night after night, without ever coming nearer. In the spring, the moon appears on the eastern horizon before the sun has disappeared in the west. She is pale; he turns a fiery red; all the breadth of the sky stretches between them."

While Aunt Sophie was telling me this primitive and brutal story, I remembered an old song; it was the lullaby that Nianka sang during our childhood:

> *The sun and the moon*
> *Were brother and sister;*
> *With love they burned,*
> *With an ardent love;*
> *In spite of their father and their mother,*
> *With an ardent love. . . .*

I had heard this song hundreds of times, and had always regarded it as something innocent and rather silly. I had paid no more attention to it than to the sound of the sea breeze that set the shutters rattling outside my window. I took it as a sort of Russian *Jack and Jill*, in which the sun played the part of Jack. I never thought of the words. Old Nianka, I remembered, had been humming them in a low voice on that famous birthday when I wished to hear nothing whatsoever. Even then, as I hurried past her door, I had been struck by the phrase "brother and sister." It was a time when my two sorrows had mingled together, and when their combined weight was more than I could bear. Sasha had deserted me; he had vanished into the clouds, and I should never see him again. But in my loneliness, help had come to me from the skies; I had thought that the green parrot would be my confidant, my consoler, my friend, my all—a living being to speak to and be answered! I had thought he would be mine. . . .

And when the sorrow of losing my bird was added to that of having lost my brother, I wished to die.

Aunt Sophie did not perceive that she was preaching to a convert when she spoke of this love passing all reason. She had formed a rather imaginary ideal of passion; she confessed that for her part she had felt nothing of the sort toward my late uncle.

"And how was it," I asked her, "that for all your indulgence to the memory of Alexander and Maria Serguyevna, you never forgave my own parents, who were only cousins?"

"But we forgave them," she said. "They never forgave us! After your grandfather's death, we wrote and begged them to come home. We have been writing them every year, and they never answer! When your father comes to Russia on business, he lives in St. Petersburg with friends whom we don't even know by sight. He spends whole months there without ever coming to Gatchina, where his mother has been waiting for all these years. It was Sasha's death that put an end to all hopes of reconciliation. When their son was born, your parents thought that Heaven was blessing their union. This fine heir was their answer to the paternal curse. The moment they

lost him, your grandfather wrote and said that
God had spoken."

&

When a little child comes into the world, it is
beyond reproach. At first one cannot even tell
what will be the color of its eyes, of its hair.
Within it, all the possibilities of the race are hidden, just as intoxication, crime, and madness are
hidden in the grape that ripens in the dew. We
are born at the mercy of our heredity. If this were
a single monster tyrannizing over us, our lot
would be enviable, but instead it consists of
many forces that war against one another; and
since we ourselves are placed at the intersection
of the lines, we are the predestined scene of the
accident. How could this brother and sister have
failed to love each other? In the skein of our family, there are two colors, which have formed
many shades; in the river of our family, there are
two currents which sometimes intermingle,
sometimes flow separately, but which are never
lost. The difference between them is as sharp as
that between hot and cold or light and dark.

Years ago, when I gave a black husband to
Koshka, my white cat, her children were born
spotted. Then, in the children of her children, I
found a gray kitten. It was the feeblest of them
all. It could never make up its mind; it was incapable of sucking its mother's breast, of miaow-
ing, and even of opening its eyes. I think it died
of indecision. In the third generation, there was
a little pure-white male and a little black female.
If I had followed the variations of this family of
cats much farther, doubtless I should have seen
the immaculate Koshka reappearing in one of
her great-granddaughters, and Koshka's black
mate in one of the little males, the son of her
grandson.

My own family was divided between light and
dark types in much the same fashion. In the beginning, a young man of the South must have
fallen in love with a young woman of the North,
or vice versa. These two must have felt the violent attraction that brings opposites together. In
their descendants, the opposing races struggled
for victory: there were spotted souls, more white

than black, others more black than white, and unhappy gray souls. But once the two currents triumphed completely in the same generation, and in two individuals of the opposite sex, the dark brother and the blonde sister would be fated to feel an irresistible passion for each other—the passion to which Maria and Alexander had succumbed.

Though human laws forbade them to love, their blood was stronger than any law. A madness that was higher than human wisdom ordered their bodies to be joined together. When they could not obey their blood, one of them died and the other lost her reason.

Merely by seeing the miniatures of Maria Serguyevna and her brother in the oval box, I knew that they were relatives only in name, and that they were pure representatives of two wholly different races. Victims of their blood and of their time, they were not the children of one father and mother, but two predestined lovers.

What would have happened to me if Sasha had lived?

CHAPTER X

MARIE, TOO,

SEES THE GREEN PARROT

ON THE TWENTY-SIXTH of July, 1914, at Roehampton, my husband had a fall that stretched him unconscious between the broken legs of his favorite pony. The horse was shot on the scene of the accident; the rider expired the following day in Chelsea Hospital without having recovered his senses.

My widowhood began in the tumult of the Austrian declaration of war against Serbia. Three months later I entered the Russian hospital at Cannes, which my father-in-law had founded, just as one enters a convent. My black veil, which caused me to be taken for a war widow, when I was merely a polo widow, was exchanged for the white veil of a nurse. I devoted myself solely to anesthesia. My domain was that of the unconscious; I brought sleep to the wounded. In the operating room, I appeared only at certain hours, armed with a file to strike off the head of the chloroform vials, and carrying ethyl chloride, morphine, and ether, with a mask in my hand. I was glad that my presence put people to sleep, that I approached men only to induce a state of insensibility.

After twenty-two months of service, weary of having given rest so often, I went to Biarritz on leave, under the orders of my physician. My lassitude was the excuse for my trip. My real reason was a letter from Mlle. Vignot which contained the disturbing news of her departure and asked me to take care of Marie.

My sister was threatened by a plot that Olga had woven about her. The trouble-maker had succeeded in convincing my mother that Marie had compromised herself with a golf instructor, a man of forty, a Swede with a questionable reputation who had introduced himself into the bosom of my family under the pretense of laying out a golf links on our own grounds—an idea that was calculated to find favor with parents like ours, who preferred to remain at home and liked to have their children under their eyes.

A letter had been found in Marie's room. It was in the handwriting of the golf instructor and revealed a happy lover. Olga had played the part of informer, and Mlle. Vignot affirmed that the letter really belonged to her. But my mother, who ordinarily showed no interest in what her daughters were doing, had taken the part of Olga, whose tantrums frightened her, against Marie, who was defended by the governess. Only Mlle. Vignot's departure had put an end to this conflict of authority. Overwhelmed by injustice, and confessing herself powerless to combat it, she had written me before resigning the place she had occupied for nearly twenty years; she conjured me to save Marie, the victim of Olga's perfidy. I hastened to obey the voice which had so often been that of my conscience. I knew my family too well not to fear them; once the French governess had left the house, good sense had abandoned it.

An event which had been foreseen by the wis-

dom of the governess occurred before my arrival.
To brave the fate that made her ugly, to prove
that she could please and that although Marie's
beauty entitled her to the rôle, she herself would
be the romantic heroine of the two, Olga had fled
with the golf instructor.

Her scandalous departure had at least the good
result of freeing Marie from the presence of an
envious sister; Olga hated her for the very reason
that made me love her: because she was she and
Marie was I.

❧

I had not seen my parents since the beginning
of the war. I found them at the same point where
I had left them: the situation was unchanged,
one might say. My mother considered the mon-
strous event as she considered everything else:
from the angle in which she had been placed by
the death of her son. Every day, after reading the
papers, she spent hours with my father and Aunt
Alix discussing what would have happened if
Sasha had lived. They considered all the possibilities and chose the most contradictory hy-

potheses: sometimes he would have led Russia in the way of progress by means of a wise liberalism; sometimes he would have been the firm support of the wavering autocracy which alone, by its return to the sacred principle of absolute power, could save his country. They imagined twenty different careers for him: would he be a cabinet minister, the governor of St. Petersburg, the private secretary of the Czar, a councilor of the Russian embassy in Paris? They counted his years. At present he was thirty-four; with his name, and with the rapid promotions of wartime, he would be a brigadier-general already; soon he would be a lieutenant-general. Sometimes they pictured him as having enlisted in the armies of the country where he was born; by the end of the war he would be a marshal of France, like Poniatowski. At other times he was an aviator, a rival of Garros, Guynemer, and Fonck.

"He would be a man of his time," sighed my mother.

Or perhaps, to please Aunt Alix, he would have joined the British navy; with Admiral Jellicoe, he would have sunk the German fleet; he would have opened the Dardanelles; he was the conqueror of Constantinople.

They showed us on the map how the Allies had blundered at Gallipoli, and how Sasha would have repaired the mistakes of the other leaders, or still better, how he would have prevented these mistakes. When the question of sending Japanese troops to Europe was being discussed, my mother's imagination took fire. Sasha left Constantinople, where he had heard a mass of victory in St. Sophia's. He went to persuade the Mikado that he should embark for Toulon at the head of his troops. Sasha would cut the Kaiser's throat with his Japanese saber.

After these glorious days came days of sorrow. Wouldn't Sasha be wounded? When she heard people speaking of parents who had received no word from their sons for a year, my mother remembered that she too had been a long time without news of her boy. Then she would stir restlessly in her invalid's chair; she became irritable; her patience was at an end. What could have

116

happened to Sasha? Why didn't he write? She felt that her son was among the missing.

In the hospital, I often heard soldiers who had lost a limb describe the sufferings they felt in their amputated members. If a nurse set down something heavy, a tray or a basin for example, on the part of the bed they still believed to be occupied by the lost hand or foot, they cried out in pain.

In the same way, my mother's feelings continued to flow toward the child she no longer possessed. She really suffered from the imaginary accidents that threatened this flesh of her flesh, which, nourished for long years by her constant thoughts, had not ceased to live and stir within her. Condemned by her passion to bear this cherished son forever, she continued his endless gestation; the movements of her child disturbed her unceasingly; her burden was a ghost, and she could never be delivered. The child she carried in her womb had grown, had become a man. One felt that she was overburdened by the weight of the intruder. He lived at the cost of her reason;

the more he was present, the more absent she became. It seemed to me that I was seeing the soul of my mother deformed by the fruit of her love, and, out of shame and filial piety, I turned my eyes away from this painful spectacle.

No, nothing had changed in my home since I was a child; my parents' thoughts followed the same course. Recent misfortunes had left no trace in their minds; autumn rains do not raise the level of the sea. And yet their eldest daughter, Anne, had died in Russia after a long and cruel illness; the second, Elizabeth, had become insane after being deserted, and was now dragging out her life in a Swiss sanatorium. I had lost the husband they gave me; Olga, the next-to-last, had made what was called "a bad marriage." They had cast her off, and, what was more to my sorrow, it was because of her that Mlle. Vignot had been forced to leave the household.

When I came back to live with my parents, the brief tempest raised by Olga's elopement had already died away. They never spoke of her; already she was forgotten. All the household continued to breathe the same air lacking in density and warmth, the moral atmosphere of the tomb. They were still oppressed by the feeling of emptiness which had reigned since the death of Sasha. I perceived that Marie, like myself in other days, suffered visibly from the lack of tenderness. She knew she had no place in the hearts of her parents, who were wholly absorbed in their thoughts of another. She too suffered from the impossibility of making herself loved by them —the disease which had once attacked my soul, and which had induced me to shower all my affection on a bird.

When I saw Marie, I rediscovered the vein of my ancient feelings, and explored it to learn how far my sister had progressed. Had she seen the green parrot, or did she still live in ignorance of her fate? Had the man who eloped with Olga appeared to her as a promise of happiness? Had she thought that she loved him?

"She will confess only to you," Mlle. Vignot had written me. "You must begin by restoring her faith in those about her. Regain her confidence, or rather resuscitate it, for this feeling was killed in Marie's heart by Olga's treachery."

I approached Marie, soothing her with my voice and my hand as if she were a high-tempered young animal. Each day after luncheon, I led her either to the deserted beach that extended to the foot of our house, or else to the end of the park, under the pines which had grown during my absence. Only there did we find each other once more.

At luncheon, my mother in her chaise-longue would have a whole side of the table to herself. The rest of us felt a little crowded by comparison. A glacial silence descended on us all, though at long intervals my father and Aunt Alix would exchange a few remarks about the weather. The next hour was devoted to reading the newspapers, an occupation that led invariably to the same conversations. Out of consideration for my mother, Aunt Alix, too, had begun to ramble. One day I heard her saying, "I carried some flowers to Sasha; today is the dear boy's birthday."

The only birth commemorated in my parents' house was that of their dead son!

I could no longer bear these aberrations. I escaped, taking my sister with me. We ran down the steps of the terrace. By reaction, we burst into laughter as soon as we were alone; we held each other's hands and whirled round till we were dizzy; we rubbed our heads together amicably; I rested my chin on the back of her neck and we stood for some moments in this position, as we had seen young horses do. The innocent animal-like joy that we shared brought us together more than mutual confidences would have done. The ten years between us had ceased to count; Marie at eighteen and I at twenty-eight were of the same height, the same weight; and if we both reacted like boarding-school girls, it was because life had made us eternal adolescents.

Before my return to Biarritz, I had feared to find Marie with the changed disposition that can be observed among animals as well as people: as soon as they fall in love, they lose their gayety, they cease to play. But Marie had retained all of her joyous verve.

I understood her without asking for explanations: Mlle. Vignot's fears were unjustified. The Swedish adventurer who eloped with Olga had left Marie untroubled. The jealous sister's triumph over the beautiful sister had been only imaginary. She had foolishly abandoned herself to the clutches of her own prey, thinking that she was snatching him from a rival. Marie had not fallen in love; her feelings were not even affected; and I was as sure of this as if she had declared it upon oath. She had attached herself to no one, and since I had long since detached myself from everything, we were in harmony; the rhythms of our two lives were the same. From this came our perfect understanding.

Besides, Marie and I were of the same blood, the same complexion. Who knows to what degree physical repugnance interferes with our sentiments? The immense majority of people are distasteful to us; literally, "we can't touch them"; and a thousand reflexes warn us that we

should approach them as little as possible. Sometimes it happens that we feel a sort of intellectual
kinship toward people with whom the least
physical contact is unbearable. It also happens
that physical attraction may be accompanied
by a strong moral repugnance which, in well-
balanced individuals, interferes with the work of
the instincts. Or again, it may happen that we
develop an aversion for some quality which had
begun by inspiring our sympathy. In the end,
our own body is the only one we never find re-
pulsive. This deep and tenacious preference for
ourselves, which is born with us, which we are
afraid to confess, which never leaves us under
any circumstances, and which follows us to the
tomb, was what I felt for Marie. It was the same
sort of affection that mothers have toward their
babies. Whether this emotion of mine was a
sort of aberrant maternal love, or whether it
was inspired by my love for myself, matters very
little; in either case my tender affection for Marie was something I had never felt for another. I
approached her with delight; I touched her;

I breathed her perfume as if I were smelling a flower.

The physical sympathy I felt toward her was accompanied by a mental attraction; we discovered in other the same habits of thought, the same moral quirks. In her room, which had once been mine, I one day found her dreaming before the mirror. Marie confessed that she spent whole hours staring at herself.

"You too!" I said, carried away with tenderness.

It was an old game of mine, one I had learned from my long experience with solitude. Before we were married, my husband often teased me because he had found, so he said, that the carpet was worn away in front of my mirror. Marie had left it in no better condition.

The general opinion in the family was that both of us worshiped our own image. As proof, they repeated something I had said years before. When Mlle. Vignot paid us her first visit, before accepting the post of governess, she had asked me, "What do you do when you aren't study-ing?"—"I look at myself," was the answer.

Miss Grey had often punished me by putting a cloth over the glass in my room. When I had been good and she offered me a reward, I asked only the privilege of looking at myself.

On discovering the same contemplative habits in Marie, I formed a quite different opinion of her than my parents had formed of me. I took it as proof that she too had been left with only her-self to consult, only herself to trust.

I remembered a very old book of travels in which I once read a perhaps fantastic, but cer-tainly touching, description of an old Japanese custom. A young emperor, on his accession to the throne, was led by his priests and high dig-nitaries into seven different temples. In the first, he saw dragons; in the second, treasures; in the third, the images of former emperors, his ances-tors; in the fourth, fifth, and sixth respectively, their sacred books, their tombs, and statues of the beasts and gods they descended from. Finally, deserted by all his guides, he entered the seventh temple, where he found nothing but a little round mirror. Its meaning was, "There is nothing, after all. Count on yourself alone."

Certain of the answer she would give me, I asked Marie:

"Do you play at making yourself ugly?"

The accusation of vanity so often brought against myself did not even occur to my mind. I was only too familiar with the real nature of this long game one played with the mirror.

"Do you make faces?"

"Yes."

"Often?"

"Every night before going to bed."

To advance in the ways of perfection, this practice was better than following a self-imposed discipline. It was better than meditating in front of a death's-head like St. Francis Borgia.

These séances of self-hypnotism led farther than one might believe, and to a different goal. I had never forgotten their lesson. Beauty, that great pleasure, is at the mercy of the slightest accident; a breath is enough to destroy it, and that breath might be my own. A little swelling of the cheeks at their base, a wrinkling of the nose, a raised eyebrow, a lip turned down at the corners, and beauty had ceased to exist.

"Quit making faces, my dove," said our old nurse, who had surprised me more than once in the act of changing my looks. "God might punish you for spoiling His handiwork."

But I was ahead of Him. "Yet a little while and you shall see me no more. . . . Yet a little while and you shall see me. . . ." With the coming of wrinkles, flabby cheeks, and a double chin, people would laugh at the face which had once made them dream.

Playing hide-and-seek with oneself . . . was it not a fine amusement? In less than a second, I restored that which I had ruined. What a proof of superhuman power! My nurse's God, who put features together, worked far less rapidly. He had spent many a year in destroying one face, and then in creating it once more with the same materials. It was nearly a century since the Rose of St. Petersburg had vanished, and only now that her beauty had reappeared in you, Marie!

*

I had come to Biarritz to see whether my younger sister needed me. After a very short visit, I went back to Cannes, intending to resume my work in the hospital for a few weeks only; I would return to Marie as soon as I could find some one else to anesthetize the wounded. Soon after my departure, she wrote that our house was about to be transformed into a convalescent home for British and Russian officers. Our huge villa, now more than half empty, had attracted the attention of the local authorities; they were seeking rooms in which to lodge the new refugees, who, like driftwood, had been cast on the shores of the Gulf of Gascony by the last offensive. The house my father had built in the image of Gatchina, "to be happy in, and to have a great many children," had become too large.

Empty were the rooms of the married daughters who would never return, of the daughter who was dead, of the daughter who was mad, of the daughter who had run away! Empty were the study and the nursery; empty the governess's room and that of the old nurse, who had gone off to die in her Siberian village.

The newcomers were to be lodged in the upper story, where the children had been. Thus, my mother would not be disturbed by their presence. Their names would be submitted beforehand by the Red Cross; one would know the sort of persons one had to deal with, and could decide whether or not to invite them to the table. Then too, wasn't it everybody's duty to do what he could toward winning the war? After three years, the only sacrifices my parents had made were in their imagination. It is true, of course, that this was the dearest part of themselves. . . .

Marie was disturbed for my sake by these great changes that were taking place during my absence. Under the new conditions, would I consent to return? There was always a room for me, even if it was only hers. Besides, the Red Cross had been warned, and up till the present had announced only the discreet arrival of three colonels of the Indian Army. As for the Russians, there was no use counting on them. There were too few of them in France, and it was quite improbable that any would be sent from the Eastern front. They were merely an excuse to have three flags floating from the Italianate roof of our house: the French, the English, and the Russian, all of them uniting, without blending, the same colors in different arrangements.

The promised colonels were late in appearing. I felt a little impatience in Marie's letters.

One morning they arrived! From that day, her letters reflected a sort of joyous animation. There was company in the house, something that had never been seen before.

I learned that the colonels were old bachelors, retired officers who had reëntered the service in 1914. One of them, Fairfax, had lost an arm; an-

other, Frazer, had lost a leg; the third, Colonel
Gordon, combined the misfortunes of his two
comrades, having lost both a leg and an arm. All
three suffered from rheumatism of the joints;
they were waiting to resume their posts on the
General Staff. Though they could have returned
to England, they did not wish to leave France,
their fatherland "for the duration."

While waiting to proceed with their plans of
attack, they played chess all day, and Marie
learned the game. In her letters, she spoke of her
new friends in terms drawn from the language of
our childhood: "The colonels are perfect ducks
. . . the colonels are angels . . . the colonels are
nice doggies." They were a great distraction for
her. . . . What she failed to see, and what I
easily imagined, was the great distraction she
must have been for them.

After a few weeks, the tone of her letters
changed. The colonels were no longer so nice.
They argued; they tyrannized over her, and
though she was so anxious not to do anything to

irritate them, she angered first one, then another, by nothing at all, by a thoughtless word, by beginning a game of chess with the one she found in the drawing room, while another, "whose turn it was," would be waiting for her on the terrace.

The "perfect ducks" became owls; the "nice doggies" bit; the "angels" fell from grace and turned into devils. Marie was at the end of her wits; she wondered, "Is it because the rainy weather affects their rheumatism? Or does the sea air excite them?"

At the hospital from which they had come, they were nicknamed "Orestes and the two Pylades." In Africa and India, as in Scotland, they were more than brothers in arms; they had been hunting and fishing companions. They had killed together, and nothing creates a more lasting friendship. At first they had seemed full of respect and affection for one another. What was the cause of their present quarrel?

Marie's astonishment was touching. She had not yet realized that the usual effect of her pres-

ence on men would be to dissolve their friendships, as mercury dissolves gold. She wrote me:

> Their ill-temper is incredible. Just imagine,
> Colonel Frazer began a sort of hunger-strike yes-
> terday, merely because Aunt Alix was away and I
> had to cut the meat in poor Gordon's plate. Of
> course I had to change my place at table and sit be-
> side him. Frazer then accused me of not wishing
> to be his neighbor; he said I disliked him. I told
> him that I had believed they were all my friends,
> but now I could see that none of them really liked
> me; or rather they all liked me as if they hated
> me. . . .

Neither age nor infirmity protects men from
hope. Marie did not know as yet that the least
amiable, the most unfortunate male believes
himself to be capable of inspiring love the moment he feels it himself.

The following letter was brief, and urged me
to come home. The news from Russia was very
disturbing. My father had set out for London;
perhaps he would go to Sweden to see his business agent. The colonels, alarmed by his depar-

ture, which had thrown the house into disorder, were very much nicer, more like they had been "before." Before what? Marie did not know, did not say.

She added:

"There is a new convalescent in the house, Captain Renell Page, a nephew of Aunt Alix's."

And Marie's letter ended with these words which, I don't know why, sent a cold shiver down my spine:

"You'll see for yourself that he isn't like the others. . . ."

CHAPTER XI

RENELLINO

HE WAS not "like the others" because he was young. He had nothing in his favor except his youth, and Marie had been living among the old. It is the lot of the last-born child to arrive after the feast is over, to see the decline of things, to watch at deathbeds. For my part, I could remember my parents when they were twenty years younger, and they had aged more than I liked to realize.

People often said of Aunt Alix that she "hadn't changed a bit." This was true, and perhaps it made her case the saddest of all. One must move with a moving world; to be changeless is to become terrifying. When a beautiful face is impassive, it ceases to be charming; in the end, it frightens us. The secret of Medusa was her fixity.

By proving herself immovable, Aunt Alix was turning all of us into stone.

Everybody that surrounded my young sister was bowed with age, from our parents and their servants down to the domestic animals. She spoke of "the old doctor, the old coachman, the old bulldog, the old cook, the old fox terrier. . . ." She had also said "the old colonels."

On my return from Cannes, I met these providential guests, and I saw that she had spoken the truth: they were all old men, with the exception of Renell Page. He alone lived without showing by his hair, his temples, his eyes, his teeth, that he was preparing to die. One might have said that destiny had kept Marie from seeing a man of her own age until the day when this stripling appeared before her, adorned with youth as his one jewel. Renell Page had nothing in his favor except his twenty-two years.

He was a poor little blond young man whose sandy hair hadn't quite the strength to be red. He shivered in an army overcoat that always seemed too large. He had taken part in the war, but most of all he seemed to have taken cold. Marie and Renell Page, as I saw them from a distance, on the station platform in the midday sun—Marie and Renell Page as they must have appeared to the eyes of others—were the most ill-assorted couple in the world, the nymph and the pale stripling, Diana and her sick greyhound.

"It was because she had no choice," our family physician told me later.

This possible marriage was discussed backstairs long before it was mentioned in the drawing room. The servants disapproved of it, and their murmurs soon reached us. In a patriarchal family such as ours, their opinion was not without importance; they formed the chorus in the tragedy: *vox populi, vox Dei.* They mourned over future events; they saw the coming of troubles that rarely failed to materialize. I learned that Renell Page was called "chicken-hearted" in the kitchen. According to Ursule, the cook, he had "no more blood than a fish." Paul, the coachman, affirmed in the words of a horse-trader that he was "broken-winded," and Léon, the gardener, announced in prophetic language that he was "a bird of ill omen."

Honorine, the Basque parlor-maid, who had come back to us after a series of misadventures in love which had robbed her of all desire to laugh, was bold enough to offer Marie advice. "Why wouldn't it be better to marry the old *milord* who has such an honest look? Isn't it better to be an old man's darling than a young man's slave?" She cited my example: hadn't my life been an easy one? "But if the heart says, 'Go drown yourself,'" she added, "one must do as the heart commands."

Though Marie's state of mind was obvious, my mother was far too absent-minded to observe what had happened. She saw none of the things that "knocked your eye out," as the servants liked to say. Aunt Alix pretended to be blind. She held herself in reserve, at an equal distance from her nephew and her niece, in the attitude appropriate to a cold beauty whom even time had respected.

The colonels made me their confidante, a rôle to which I was unaccustomed. I pretended to take their advice, to heed their dire prophecies, and to warn Marie of the risk she was running. They agreed that my task was to open her eyes— which, as a matter of fact, were open already to the depths of life. But except for me, no one had realized what she was seeing. . . .

The colonels' opinion was not expressed in metaphors, like that of the servants, but it was the same: I ought to cure Marie of her infatuation for this poor stripling who had no future; Renell Page was completely unworthy of her. He was a "nobody" and he was "nothing." One of these expressions denied him the quality of having a soul; the other did not even acknowledge the existence of his body.

As for me, warned by my own experience, not caring to examine the personality of the insignificant little young man, and thinking only of Marie, I had read in my sister's eyes from the beginning that her love was great, healthy, strong, candid, and much to be feared. From that time,

I could only become its minister. I began by ridding Marie of the espionage service which had been organized by her aged suitors. She had to be rescued from the cross-fire of their glances. Discussing her problems with them served as an excuse for a series of private meetings. I took her place at the chess table; soon I revealed a real preference for bridge. This game had the advantage of occupying all three colonels at once. To keep Marie from being their target, I was creating a sort of parallel mirage: Fairfax and Frazer soon glided into another adoration. My resemblance to my sister removed the idea of infidelity, which is extremely disagreeable to most Anglo-Saxons. The change in the direction of their sentiments took place imperceptibly and with no great difficulty. I triumphed over my sister with her full consent and with her own arms: I too was blonde! Marie was grateful to me for having supplanted her, for having made a diversion that restored her liberty. Whether or not it is shared, the first effect of love is to destroy the liberty of its object.

Marie felt that she had been freed from invisible bonds, and I, who delivered her, was content to lose a freedom to which I had always been indifferent.

Only Colonel Gordon, the oldest of her three suitors, the one whom Honorine called "the old *milord*," had retained an affection that was too deep to be conquered by despair. He was one of those tall Englishmen who are ennobled by their years; he had the look of an old thoroughbred. Seeing how handsome he was in his decrepitude, I could not keep from thinking that Marie would have loved him had it not been for the forty years that stood between them. The passion he felt for her had been transformed and purified into renunciation. After expressing the lowest opinion of little Page, as his two comrades had done, and after giving vent to his sorrow at seeing Marie engaged in the adventure of her life with this good-for-nothing, this poor thing, this broken toy, he had changed his attitude, and slowly, courageously, had reached my own point of view:

namely, that we must admit the inevitable and do all we could to assist Marie in her pursuit of this poor thing, this broken toy.

Only with Gordon could I really talk of my sister's interests. I was depending on him to discover the secret of Renell Page. Incredible as it may seem, the young man had given no hint of his true feelings; we could only guess what they were. It is true that when all of us were together, he usually stood or sat beside my sister, but the attentions he paid her seemed merely the natural right of the only unmarried girl in the house. They lent each other books, and when we set out on one of our long drives, Page would lay his overcoat and cane beside the seat that was to be occupied by Marie. But the momentary impression of disunion I had felt on seeing them together for the first time was repeated more than once as the weeks passed by.

While the eyes of my young sister reflected love as clearly as a glass reflects the sun, I felt vaguely that Renell Page's glances seemed dead.

His eyes were tarnished mirrors, blind windows vainly facing the sunrise.

One evening, after a long look at him, I asked Gordon, who had been watching the young couple from his corner:

"Does he sometimes speak of her?"

"Often . . . that is, every time I mention her name."

"And what does he say?"

"Nothing: that she is 'really a charming girl.' It's just as if he said that the Parthenon was really a charming ruin, or that the Atlantic was a charming ocean."

Gordon's love was so generous that he would have liked to infuse it into this sullen, unhealthy creature, so that through Renell's opaque heart, something of his own warmth and light could have reached Marie. But little Page could neither emit rays nor transmit them. He defended himself against the light with the placidity of a night-bird closing its inner eyelids against the day. He had a way of being impenetrable that reminded me of Aunt Alix, in the days when my happiness depended on her.

"I should like to shake him," said Gordon. "Yes, I should like to give him a whipping."

And sometimes he added:

"I should like to kill him!"

He confessed to me that in the beginning he had tried to discourage Marie by revealing what he believed to be the truth about Page: that he was of feeble health, and perhaps was even threatened with tuberculosis. Gordon had taken the wrong tack, and instead of frightening Marie, he had touched her. To pity the one we love is to love him still more; we Christians pity God. I remembered my father's objection to my dear bird: that he too suffered from this infectious disease and was capable of transmitting it to me. . . .

I would infinitely rather have died from his presence than from living without him. What did this threat matter to me then? What did it matter to Marie at present?

Gordon added that he had tried another

method: he had made fun of Renell Page, and this apparently with success. Marie had encouraged him; she had even imitated Renell, to Gordon's great surprise. She had a natural talent for mockery, and moreover it is always a pleasure to discuss the one you love. How can this be done without confessing your passion, without surrendering and humiliating yourself? To make fun of him is a tempting method. And perhaps, by piercing him with this volley of harmless arrows, you are proving to your own satisfaction that he is invulnerable.

Marie had begun playing this game with me as soon as I returned; I had concluded that she herself was wounded. Gordon did not know that in my old room, which the two of us now occupied together, many hours of the night were spent in imitating little Page, in walking like him, in sitting down like him, in stepping backwards as we bowed, in pronouncing with his special accent certain phrases that were as much his own as was the shape of his hands or the pale tint of his eyes.

145

I excelled in these grotesque imitations. I had only to say, "How sad!" or "Oh, absurd!" with a certain inflection of the voice, for Marie to burst into laughter and throw her arms round my neck.

It was to thank me for being so amusing. . . . But most of all, it was to kiss a fleeting resemblance on my face. In pronouncing little Page's words, I must have made certain movements of the lips that gave my mouth, for the moment at least, the same expression as his.

She called him "Renellino" when she wished to make fun of him—in other words, when her desire to speak of him became irresistible. One evening she told me with a wry little smile:

"There's no denying it, your Renellino is a poor stick. I asked him if he thought you were pretty, and he didn't know what to answer. Finally he said, "Well! Well! Well!' and stood there like this, with his mouth open."

She stuck out her lower lip, so as to imitate the prognathism of the young Englishman.

It was her first timid attempt to learn by ruse

or deduction whether or not he thought her pretty. She had obtained no reply.

Yes, Renellino was a poor stick. Often when I looked at his little, expressionless face, I had thought of saying, "Marie loves you!" and I wondered whether he would understand.

It was lucky for me that I had fallen in love with a mere parrot. There was no need to ask what his feelings were, and to wait until they were the same as mine before declaring my passion. And doubtless it would have been better for my sister to have loved a bird, as happened with me, rather than to love a man who seemed to have no more intelligence or feeling than a bird.

But where was the cage in which, with Gordon's assistance, I could imprison Renellino, and so bring Marie her green parrot?

❧

Gordon had been acting mysteriously for some days. He drove out alone in the carriage, without telling us where he was going. His two friends, who accused him of dabbling in the occult sciences, teased him about his disappearances. They suspected him of having found, somewhere in the neighborhood, a Basque woman afflicted with second sight. They were not far from the truth: Gordon had just sent to Paris for his chiromancer, and he had been paying her a visit every afternoon.

One day he confessed his weakness to me:

"Won't you let me take you to see Mme. Duffaut, the medium?"

"What, to visit this woman who reads your hand? If you could prove to me at this very moment that my whole fortune was written in my palms, I shouldn't bother to take off my gloves. I have no desires whatsoever, and I'm no longer interested in my future."

"You are still interested in that of Marie."

"Have her go to the medium herself."

"No," he said with a serious air. "If the future predicted was not the one she hopes for, she would suffer, and I shouldn't like her to suffer."

"But I don't believe in fortune tellers!"

"Really," said Gordon, "one has to believe in them a little, and I'll try to explain why. People say that I'm always thinking about the fourth dimension. It may be that this is a frivolous occupation, but it's dear to me because it's my own, and because an old man like me has nothing to cherish but his ideas. For a great many years, I have suspected that time was only an illusion. . . ."

He added, with a melancholy smile:

"A very painful illusion to me, as you can readily guess. But although I'm quite powerless to make others change their opinions on this subject, I can at least, if I so desire, destroy the illusion in myself by an effort of the intelligence.

"It's very hard to explain these matters without either boring you or making you suspect that I've lost my mind. But I might illustrate by an example. Just imagine that you and I are riding wooden horses on a merry-go-round. To any one who watches, I precede and you follow. Before you have reached a certain point, I shall have passed it already. However, the spectator may decide to adopt a different point of view: he may say that when you reach the given point, you will have finished a revolution, while I, at the same moment, am beginning another. From this point of view, he can *predict* me, whereas he *remembers* you; I am in the future and you in the past; I am new and you are old. . . . Again, we can imagine another spectator who views the merry-go-round from above. None of these distinctions would matter to him: we should all be passing at the same time.

"Here is another image:

"Let us think of human life as a motion-picture film that is being unrolled before a projector. Our past is the part of the film that has already appeared; we remember it; our present is the part now being shown on the screen; our future is the portion still to be projected.

"What if the mechanism got out of order? What if the projector illuminated the part of your life that is plunged in the mists of the future? You would see what has never been seen.

"My medium is a broken projector. I wish to place you before her so that she can throw at least a glimmer on your future; perhaps you will see a portion of it as clearly as you see the corner of the terrace where we are sitting at this moment, in our wicker armchairs with our backs to the sea.

"To explain the nature and the limits of my sibyl's power, I shall tell you what happened to me in 1914, a few weeks before the declaration of war:

"I was spending a month in Paris. A friend who shared my interest in the psychical sciences had just introduced me to Mme. Duffaut, with whom I arranged for a private séance. At first I thought it would be a failure. She seemed so stupid and vulgar that I hardly listened to what she said. However, after nearly an hour of incoherent declamations, she began speaking clearly; I was impressed by the precision of her words. In an ordinary tone of voice, she was describing a scene that was evidently appearing before her eyes:

" 'You are making a journey; a lady whose requests you never refuse has sent for you. At present you are on a boat, but your journey is not a sea voyage. I can see you on deck with the lady. Both of you are leaning against the rail. The boat

151

tugs at its anchor. You are looking at the sea. . . . There is another lady beside you. Only one of the two ladies has sent for you, but both of them wished to see you. . . .'

"I had several projects at the moment, but none of them explained this voyage which was not a voyage at sea. At my age, it hardly seemed possible for me to be summoned by a woman whose orders I had always obeyed.

"I was not especially eager to learn the identity of the two ladies who were waiting for me on the boat that tugged at its anchor; nevertheless I had been impressed by the change in the register of Mme. Duffaut's voice when she pronounced these words.

"A month later, I was preparing to return to London. I was convinced that I had profited not in the least by my visit to the medium. However, on the eve of my departure, I received a telegram from Queen Alexandra; she was summoning me to Cherbourg, where Her Majesty was on the yacht *Victoria and Albert* with the Dowager Empress of Russia. I could not refuse the invitation.

I had spent much of my childhood in Denmark, my father having served as Queen Victoria's ambassador to the court of Christian X. I had known the King's daughters since my earliest years, and they honored me with their friendship. Accordingly I took the train for Cherbourg, where I was to have luncheon with the two Danish princesses. It was only when we were standing on the deck of the yacht, leaning against the rail, that I witnessed the scene described by Mme. Duffaut. I could not have seen it a month before, and yet it existed already. . . ."

And Gordon added:

"Your life is so closely united with that of your sister, and you love her so much, that I hope you will see part of her destiny on the same film as yours. Come and stand before my broken projector. Perhaps I shall see you on the steps of old St. Martin's with a bride, or in a Scotch castle looking through the windows at the rain falling on the acres of heather that will be Marie's estate! Then at last you can be confident of the girl's future—which, to tell the truth, is only her un-known present."

One morning Gordon drove me to Mme. Duffaut's door. The medium lived in a furnished room that she hired from an old bathing-attendant of Port-Vieux. I had been forced to wait several days for my appointment; her presence in Biarritz had become known, and every one seemed eager to glimpse the part of his film still hidden in the night to come.

"Has she an owl on her shoulder?" I said to Gordon as we drove along the shore. "If only she doesn't make me touch her cards! I have a horror of dirt; I shan't take off my gloves."

My aversion for fortune tellers had not diminished, but my desire to see part of Marie's future on the screen was stronger than my repugnance.

"She isn't a cartomancer," Gordon explained. "You must learn to distinguish. She is a chiro-mancer and a necromancer. She reads your hand and she questions the dead. In all probability, she is simply a victim of hysteria. But the interesting disease from which she suffers allows her to witness many events that are hidden from ourselves."

As I did not know whether Renell Page loved my sister, nor whether Gordon was right to consult Mme. Duffaut, I decided that two doubts were equivalent to one certainty. Perhaps when I returned from this visit to the sibyl, I should have lost, as if by miracle, the dull anxiety that gripped me each time I heard Marie singing before her mirror, as she let down her lovely hair: "Renellino . . . Renellino . . . is a poor stick!"

❧

The medium said, "You must take off your gloves."

We were alone together in a Renaissance dining room, under a hanging lamp, at a table covered with pink and yellow oilcloth. From a china fruit-dish, the face of Diane de Poitiers emerged in relief. Evidently the bathing-attendant was cooking in the next room, for the air was poisoned with the smell of garlic and burning grease. Mme. Duffaut wore a red flannel kimono, Turkish slippers, and a Spanish mantilla. She had the mouth of people who talk too much—the lips of a barber or an orator, stretched out of shape like an old garter.

Since I had come, I should have to show her my hands; I bared them on the table. She stared at them for a longish moment.

"Do you know that I speak with the dead?" she asked.

I nodded my head to show that I did. She assumed a cavernous voice, a borrowed voice that she wished to render sepulchral; it rang false in this little dining room full of flies and sunlight.

"Your dead are here. . . . I can see them all round you. . . . They are in the air you breathe."

I looked toward the closed window, which was obstructed with flower pots. "If they are in the air that I breathe here," I thought, "may God have pity on them!"

Mme. Duffaut vaticinated. Warned by Gordon, I let pass a torrent of incoherent words, a flood of metaphysical formulas, a verbal inun-

dation in which I recognized a number of familiar phrases: "Survival of the personality . . . human plane . . . divine plane . . . reincarnation
. . . redemption . . . deliverance of souls."

All at once the register of her voice changed.
I became attentive.

"Ah! you are surrounded by many dead . . . so
many that they jostle one another and fight for
standing room. . . . One spirit is brighter than
the rest; I shall tell him to approach you. . . .
He loves you . . . he is holding out his arms to
you. He is trying to put his arms round your
neck. . . . I couldn't distinguish him at first. At
present, I can see him very plainly. He is a child,
a boy of eight, who has been dead . . . twenty-
five years. He is wearing a sailor suit with a wide
collar . . . in the pocket of his blouse is a little
silver whistle. . . . But wait! Behind him stands
another, still brighter than he, and dead much
longer. He wears a uniform; he has a cross of
honor. . . . On his breast is a bunch of white
roses. He is addressing you in a language I can't

understand; he speaks a name that is not yours, but one he has given you, a name I can't pronounce . . . A-da . . . as-ta. . . ."

A flame darted through my mind: Astarte! This was the name Alexander Dalgorukin had given in his letters to the sister he so passionately loved. And Sasha was calling me by this name!

Tears rose to my eyes. I had inherited this dream from my mother, and at present I was weeping because some one had explained it.

The medium, as if my emotion had cast a light on the difficult text that she was deciphering slowly, continued her reading in a calmer voice:

"He could not live, and he so wished to live! It was because of you, or another like you, that he did not live. His reincarnation will take place through you. Only in this manner can he return to the human plane and accomplish his interrupted destiny. . . . He has kept you till now . . . till the *other* comes. . . ."

"Are you speaking of Marie?"

My question must have produced a sudden change in the direction of the medium's thoughts. I heard her sob. Then she continued in a different voice, as if she were telling an amusing anecdote:

". . . They are strolling in a little wood. The grass is full of flowers. I can see thousands and thousands of daisies and primroses. . . . Ah, but the grass is green! He steps up to her. . . . Without a by-your-leave, without a single word, he has kissed her right on the mouth, and his hat has fallen off. . . . Haha! Haha!"

The medium began to laugh, as if something she could not formulate was amusing her secretly. . . .

When Gordon, who had been waiting in the carriage for more than an hour, saw my changed face and my red eyes, he assumed that I had heard an evil prophecy about Marie; he thought only of her.

"Not at all," I told him. "If we can believe Mme. Duffaut, Marie is loved. She is going to be kissed in a little wood by some one who says not a single word."

"But in that case, why have you been crying?"

"I cried because the broken projector worked both ways; it cast a light on a distant past which I thought was forgotten. The medium spoke of Sasha. She even described the suit he was buried in; she mentioned his blouse and his collar; she *saw* a little silver whistle that I know is in his coffin. . . ."

And I explained briefly to Gordon that Sasha was an exceptionally gifted brother whom I had lost when I was very young. . . .

My having visited the medium proved that I could not make up my mind about Renell Page's attitude toward Marie. And every night she questioned me at length. Sitting cross-legged at the foot of my bed, her index finger against her chin and her lovely hair streaming over her shoulders, she was the little girl that every woman becomes at night, till the final morning when she wakes to find that she has been transformed during her sleep into a hollow-lipped, unkempt old crone.

Marie weighed all her chances and asked me to weigh them with her; she painstakingly recapitulated all the little events of the day, hoping that together we could come upon their meaning. Renellino had made such and such a gesture, had said such and such a thing, had given her such and such a look; he had spoken of his mother, of his dogs, of his old castle in Scotland; he had spoken of nothing at all. . . . Was it a good or a bad sign? Until this time I had never realized that the word "insignificant," which applied so exactly to little Page, could be used in a cruel sense; not to signify is almost the same as not to live; and except in Marie's deluded eyes, this young man had no significance. Did he love her? Was he indifferent to her? Vainly she sought the aid of my experience: I never dared to tell her that when I loved, when for the first and last time in my life I desired a living creature, this creature was a bird, and I had cared very little whether my feelings were reciprocated. My green parrot had one great advantage over hers: I had felt no desire to interpret his words, and I was sure of pleasing him merely by scratching his head. If I had so chosen, I could have taught him endlessly to repeat, always in the same tone of voice, "I love you, I love you"—the only words that a woman in love is eager to hear.

How many nights did I not dream of making Marie happy! By the postman's path, I was approaching the house. I carried a great circular perch of painted wood. There was a heavy chain hanging from the pedestal on which the perch rested. I attached this chain to little Page's wrist and, in my dream, I offered the whole as a gift to my sister, feeling certain that her bird would never escape!

⁂

Ever since the medium had spoken of the kiss in the little wood, I had plucked up my courage; I affirmed that I had seen Renellino's dead eyes sparkle when he looked at my sister, and I declared that his stupid reserve was merely a pretense. Gordon reassured me, and conspired with me to reassure Marie. He had come to long ardently for something which he would naturally have feared.

Since he loved her, he readily convinced himself that she was loved by Renellino. Besides, he could not imagine that a man who was subject like other men to the force of gravity and all the laws of physics, could long resist the attraction of Marie. It was merely the prudence inspired in him by a rightful feeling of his own unworthiness which had kept Renellino from declaring himself. Our anxieties were unjustified; when the moment came, the timid young man would act.

Already I was unconsciously contributing to the realization of the part of the film that the medium had revealed to me; I was helping to create the future. I had obtained Aunt Alix's permission to harness our old ponies to her old dog-cart. When we went out driving, I took the colonels in a hired landau, while Marie and Renellino occupied the ancient vehicle in which there was only room for two. Dozens of little woods exist near Biarritz. On one point, however, my mind was not at rest: it was autumn, and the medium had described a spring landscape; the projector had shown primroses and daisies in the grass.

One morning our whole family was terrified by a telegram from Stockholm. My father, on his way home from Finland, had been taken ill. He was asking me to hasten to his side so that he could dispose of some important business affairs; he had instructed his confidential agent to meet me in London, and he was giving me full power to act on his behalf. I was to have a locksmith open the cabinet in which his private papers were filed. Certain of the bonds he kept in Biarritz would have to be sold through his broker in London.

I alone was present when his private cabinet was opened. It contained the portion of our fortune that could still be saved. From an iron box, I drew several bundles of colored paper and counted them over. A photograph that had been hidden between two piles of French bonds fell to the floor.

"Sasha," I thought.

I was not in the least surprised to find him there. His picture was everywhere in the house; why shouldn't it be in this iron box where my father had hidden the remnants of his fortune? But . . . it was Sasha in a costume I had never seen before. This boy was dressed in a sort of gray uniform that buttoned on the left side. He seemed to be at least fourteen years old. Why, it couldn't possibly be Sasha. . . .

*

My mother made no objection to my departure, although it was taking place at the time of the equinoctial gales, and under dangerous conditions. She did nothing but sigh:

"When a man has no son! . . . Ah! if Sasha had only lived. . . ."

This litany which had echoed through my childhood was as familiar to my ears as the responses of the mass. I was hearing it for the last time.

The day before I left Biarritz, Gordon said to me:

"New worries must be waiting for you in Stockholm; I hope you aren't leaving any behind. Page told me last week that he had asked his mother to join us here. Since I know Lady Page, I decided to write her myself. Her answer came this morning: she says that she will be here to spend Christmas with her son."

According to Gordon, it must have been Renell Page's wish to stay with Marie that had led him to abandon his trip to Scotland. I was of the same opinion. And, when I told the news to my sister, I found it easy to convince her that Gordon and I were right. I inspired her with our own conviction: Renellino was ceasing to be a poor stick and was catching fire!

Fool that I proved to be! I was leaving Marie behind me, defenseless, lonely, at the mercy of an increasing hope. . . .

CHAPTER XII

"I WISHED TO DIE"

FAIRFAX and Frazer escorted me to Boulogne. They would have liked to go farther, but they could not enter Sweden, a neutral country. Even without their uniforms, their crutches would have betrayed them everywhere as belligerents.

I wasted several days in London, waiting to hear that the Norwegian steamer which was to carry me to Bergen had docked in Newcastle. My father's confidential agent had been unable to meet me. And, as everybody thought I was in Sweden, I received no letters from Biarritz.

It was only on the thirtieth of November, in a thick fog, that I embarked with my maid on the *Jupiter*, a Noah's ark of the neutrals, protected against torpedoes by one of the frail international conventions that still survived, though nobody knew how or why, on the sea of the universal deluge.

When I reached Stockholm, I found that my father had died a week before. I was expecting the news, and I was filled with regret at having come. Had I not been wrong to leave Marie, the only person in the world who really needed me? Why had I come to this distant city? To carry securities which had lost their value to a man who had lost everything, even life? To read a name and two dates on a tomb, in a foreign cemetery?

"Let the dead bury their dead," says the Gospel.

My father had accustomed me since childhood not to depend on him. When his vague features disappeared forever, I remembered only their years of increasing pallor, their slow obliteration. He had voluntarily cut himself off from the world; he had borne a famous name that was now extinct, without his having added to its luster. Lacking a son to continue his work, he had undertaken nothing; unable to survive himself, he had scarcely lived.

When I was a child, I had feared him as one fears sorrow; later I had pitied him without being able to love him; and the grief I felt at his death was part of an old grief I was now incapable of reviving.

I suffered remorse of a sort for having obeyed a duty that was purely formal. My father never had anything to say to me, and he had died without breaking his silence. None of the reasons that had led me to make the trip seemed valid on my arrival. I was without letters from Marie, and could hardly hope for any. To the disorder of war was added that of revolution. I had reached its ominous borders, and a thousand difficulties would face me before my return.

My father's agent, whom I found in the hospital where my father died, had taken his bed and his place; he too was dying. He had waited for me before breathing his last, so he told me, adding that he did not wish to render his soul to God before having rendered his accounts to me. To what end, since his superintendence had ceased with the property superintended, and since the paternal fortune existed no longer?

He gave me a receipt for a little hoard of jewels and precious objects which had been saved from the pillage of Gatchina through the prudence of Aunt Sophie and my grandmother, who had given him their treasures a few hours before a crowd of drunken sailors invaded the music room where these ladies were playing a Mozart sonata for four hands. They had been arrested, carried off in a motor lorry to Petrograd, and nobody knew what had become of them.

Our family treasures, rescued by M. Bobinski at the peril of his life, were at present deposited in the vaults of a Stockholm bank, the name of which he gave me. He added the address of Mme. Soltikov, a friend of my father's, who had watched at his deathbed and arranged for the funeral services.

I went to see this lady, whom I did not know, and whose name I had never heard. I found her with her old husband and her mother-in-law. All three were lying side by side in a dingy hotel room. This interior gave me a first glimpse of the existence led by refugees.

Mme. Soltikov, her eyes haggard, her clothing elegant and disordered, had the air of being a rich traveler who had just escaped from a railway accident. She greeted me with mad excitement, as if she had always known me, as if she had been impatiently waiting for my arrival. Having embraced me, she asked me at once, in the name of all she had done for my father, if I was the angel who had come to save her life. She begged me to take her son to France, her darling Felix.

Did I know the whole story? But she was forgetting: of course I couldn't know it, having come too late. She would have to tell me everything.

Felix, it seemed, had a sacred mission to perform: he was to rescue the Czar, whom the Bolsheviks were holding in prison at Tobolsk. He was to save the life of the Lord's anointed. Felix was marked for this deliverance. It was his duty to redeem the blood which had once been shed by one of his ancestors. . . . A Romanov had perished; a Romanov must now be saved. This could only be accomplished by a young man with a clean soul, who had never known sin. And so the curse would be lifted. . . . Felix was only twenty, and "He is a saint," his mother affirmed.

He had just been made an officer when the revolution broke out. Having been interned, he could leave Sweden only in disguise and with a false passport. He was expected in China; he was expected in Siberia. He must hasten to Tobolsk by sea and land. My father had done everything possible to aid hm, but the poor man had died before he had time enough to put his own plans into execution. Felix, disguised as a girl, was to pass for my lady's maid, or rather for her daughter, since it seemed I had taken my own maid with me to Sweden. Fortunately she was old!

On reaching England, he was to abandon his disguise and assume a borrowed name. The Swedish government had kept his papers, as is customary with prisoners of war, and accordingly he had been given two forged passports, one in the name of my maid, the other in our own name. The young man with whom I returned to France was to pass himself off as the minor son of my deceased father; once on Allied territory, Felix would become my brother; he would merely have to cut his hair, which was very long at present, and to resume male clothing.

I was shown his passports; they had been prepared with the aid of a consul who was under obligations to Mme. Soltikov and my father. One of them had been delivered in the name of Mlle. Alphonsine Perruchot, daughter of the widow Perruchot, my lady's maid, and on this I saw the face of a young servant. On the other I saw the photograph of the false Sasha. He was wearing the gray uniform of a Russian schoolboy, and he had the look of a child. . . .

❧

I had to prepare for our departure unaided. In the meantime, I was visiting the Soltikovs as little as possible, so as not to compromise both families. Felix had been sent to my hotel. When I saw him for the first time, his hair was gathered in a knot. He was wearing a traveling toque of suède, and a pinch-waisted coat of dark fur that fell to his ankles. Almond-eyed and delicately modeled, he resembled the Buddhas of ambiguous sex whose faces are like those of Annamite soldiers or nursemaids from Brittany. He took his meals with the servants, and though he swept out my room every day, he rarely entered it except when I was absent.

I explained to the manager of the hotel that Alphonsine Perruchot had nursed my father during his last illness; out of gratitude I was taking her back with me to France. My old lady's maid formed a real affection for this sudden daughter, and protected Felix against his own mistakes. At the same time, with her native prudence, she disguised her attentions as a sort of gruff tenderness.

Felix scarcely opened his mouth for fear of being betrayed by his voice. Besides, he was taciturn by nature. On one occasion, however, when he had to move a picture of Marie before placing the breakfast tray on the table, he remarked:

"Tell me, do all pretty women travel with their own photographs?"

"Insolent young creature!" I replied. "Let me inform you that the picture to which you refer is that of my youngest sister."

Afterwards we often smiled at each other, but we never spoke. The widow Perruchot, however, kept me in touch with her daughter's progress. It seemed that she was doing full justice to her meals; in fact, she ate almost enough for a dragoon and far too much for a servant girl. Fortunately the northerners who gathered in the kitchen were accustomed to the hearty appetites of cold climates, and so their suspicions were not aroused.

I waited five weeks before being given permission to remove my father's effects from the bank. There remained the problem of leaving Sweden with my grandmother's sapphires, which were now Marie's only dowry. It was a time when every country was trying to stop the hemorrhage of riches from which Europe had begun to suffer. After standing in line day after day in a dozen government bureaus, I was finally authorized to set out for France with my philosopher's stones, which I should have to change into gold. And still I was forced to linger. My father's poor agent had just died, and must be buried with the religious chants of the East. One had to wait one's turn at the Greek Orthodox church at Stockholm; so many Russians were dying!

Finally I left Sweden. On the twenty-eighth of February I embarked at Bergen with my two lady's maids, the mother and the daughter. They carried the three valises in which was our whole patrimony. In spite of the threatening look of the sea, the boat was full of passengers. We slept fully clothed in a cabin "For Ladies Traveling Alone," and managed to defend the fourth berth victoriously against the assaults of a middle-aged business man who claimed that his special passport gave him the right to enter.

On the first day, the storm rose. We lay almost

inanimate behind curtains that were furiously
shaken by the pitching and rolling of the vessel.
The ideas that traversed my mind during the
voyage were almost all concerned with Marie,
and they were lugubrious.

What news would I hear on reaching London?
I tried to imagine that she was happy, but I was
far too miserable myself. Little by little, as I lost
my own instinct of self-preservation, my sister's
prospects grew darker. Like all people who suffer
from the sea, I wished to die, and I ceased to believe in Marie's happiness as my own desire to live
faded away. Renell Page did not love her . . .
could not love her. . . . Beauty was good for
nothing . . . was not an argument . . . was not
even a thing in itself, and never passed a certain
degree of longitude. Was I able to judge whether
one Kaffir woman was prettier than another?
Could I choose between two Eskimos? My husband had neglected me for a woman without
looks—yes, for twenty women without looks!
. . . "Women's beauty is not in their face, as they
falsely believe; it exists only in men's minds,"

some one who wished to humiliate me had told me long before.

I implored the submarine or the drifting mine to put an end to my torture; I envied the fate of Kitchener; at each new wave that opened on the abyss, I annihilated myself with Marie. . . .

On landing at Newcastle, I recovered my taste for life. We passed the customs without any trouble, thanks to the diplomatic visa given me by the English minister to Sweden. He was a polo player, and had granted me his protection in memory of the good teammate whose prestige was still attached to my name.

In the express from Newcastle to London, my ideas changed. They were deformed by the speed of the train. I imagined that Marie's engagement had been announced; her marriage had taken place before she heard of my father's death and went into mourning. . . . She had received my telegrams; she would be waiting for me at Boulogne; she was waiting for me in London; I should see her in three hours, in two hours, in a moment. . . . Renellino was with her. He stood beside her, still shivering in the army overcoat that always seemed too large. His collar was turned up; his face was pale, his nose pointed, and he was saying:

"Well! Well! Well! Oh, absurd!"

.   .   .   .

The telegram had been sent by Aunt Alix and was dated March 3: MARIE DIED SUDDENLY COME BACK.

It was four days old. Under it was a heap of letters, almost all of them in Marie's handwriting; they contained an account of the meaningful little events that had taken place since my departure; they were meant to convince me that her happiness was approaching, and if I had not held the telegram in my hand, the torture of hope would have continued. But at present I too had second sight; I had witnessed the end of the drama without knowing all the amusing little complications that crowded the last act.

*

From one of Gordon's letters, I learned what I would have given my life not to hear. Olga had come back shortly after my departure. She had returned unexpectedly, like the traitors who appear on the stage shortly before the end of a tragedy. They say nothing, but their mere presence is a warning that the heroine is about to die. The man whose accomplice Olga had become without profit to herself, had sent her to keep watch on the inheritance even before they heard of my father's death. She had overheard an unlucky conversation between Lady Page and Aunt Alix, and had learned the secret which none of us had been able to guess. It was a poor little secret after all: if Renell Page did not love Marie, it was because he loved another. . . . This other was a Spanish girl, a professional dancer—"An immoral creature," Lady Page had said, "several years older than himself. He met her before the war."

This woman had just come from Spain; she had taken a flat in Bayonne, and he was to marry her within a few weeks. He had asked his mother to procure his father's consent to the match. Lady

Page had come to Biarritz with the intention of yielding to the inevitable.

She had hoped that the war would change her son's ideas, but the war, alas! had changed nothing whatsoever. Though apparently so weak, this young man had proved strong enough to be faithful. And who among us could reproach him for his constancy? Did he love a woman who was totally unworthy? The accusation might just as well have been turned against Marie: Renell Page was unworthy of the love she bore him.

The torture of loving is so great that no one is worthy of it; love, in reality, is always unmerited.

How joyously Olga must have broken the news to Marie! To scratch out her lovely eyes would have been no greater bliss than merely to open them. Olga lost no time. Gordon had noticed that the two sisters rarely spoke, but one day he saw Olga approach Marie and lead her away for a stroll in the garden with a confidential look. Feeling some apprehension, he followed them at a distance. The two sisters held a short conversation; then he saw Marie go running off toward the beach, and heard Olga screaming after her:

"Your Renellino doesn't want you . . . will never want you! It's no good throwing yourself at his head . . . at his head! . . ."

And the sea wind had carried her words to the terrace, where my mother sat dreaming, indifferent to all the noises of the world.

That same day, Marie made up her mind; she had written me her brief letter of farewell. It was only a page in length, very simple, yet very enigmatic, and it contained the word "wished" repeated several times:

"Don't be sorry if I'm not there, and pray for me; I *wished* to die. . . . Tell Mother that I *wished* to die. . . . I did what was right and what I *wished* to do. . . ."

Why had she repeated this word? Was it because she knew that her wishes were always mine?

She waited until Lady Page and her son had

gone away; she waited another week for news of my coming. Olga, thinking she had decided to make the best of it, was looking gloomy. The two sisters were not on speaking terms. Marie had confided in nobody. Gordon, who had seen her burst into tears when she thought she was unobserved, urged Aunt Alix to take her to Venice; he had a house there which was standing empty. Sending her away from Biarritz might have saved her, but nobody took the trouble. She should not have stayed a day longer in the place where her dreams of happiness had ceased to dwell. I had been sent to Cannes after losing my green parrot; I had recovered during my absence. . . .

One afternoon when all the family had gathered on the terrace, as they usually did on the first warm days, a messenger brought the telegram announcing my arrival. Marie excused herself, saying that she was going to Gordon's room for a new set of chessmen which had just arrived from England. She did not return. She had slipped out of the house by the servants' door—by the same

183

door that her nurse had used long ago, when Marie had to be taken for her airings without being seen by her heartbroken mother.

She carried Gordon's service revolver along with her. A little later, the group on the terrace heard a shot that seemed to come from the little wood of pines overlooking the beach. My mother had said in her wailing voice:

"But I told the gardener time and again not to shoot at the gulls!"

Marie had gone off to die in the corner of the park, near the very spot where I had tried to hang myself nineteen years before.

❧

And now I could hardly forgive her for the love I had borne her. I could hardly forgive myself for not being dead. A confused idea of retribution was taking shape in my head: Marie had merely carried out the decision I had made when I was nine years old. The demon that pursued us both, having loosened his grip on one, had clutched the other, and our strange twinship had ended. If I had died on the day when I lost the green par-

184

rot, perhaps she would have lived. I had been protected by my very immaturity, by the forces of growth within me, but Marie had possessed no such defense. And I, her sister, had deserted her at an age when growth had ended, and when passion could seize upon all the forces of her being.

Born of a mother without resignation, we refused to accept disappointment. We had lost the one thing we desired; we were incapable of forming other wishes; and something that might be called our obstinacy of heart not only removed all prospects of happiness from our future, but even abolished that future itself.

Marie had discovered her own inability to change, a weakness that excludes one from life. Although my mother had gone on living after she lost Sasha, it was only because she nourished hopes of recovering her idol, of conceiving him anew. This mirage had carried her from delusion to delusion, from youth to age, from sanity to madness. And her aberrations, by giving her back the one she loved, had preserved her existence.

No mirage had come between Marie and the sight of her misfortune. The cage and the bird had been snatched from her hands at the last moment, as from mine. And it had all happened quite simply: a few words had sufficed to kill her . . . but what bitter words they were!

PART THREE

FELIX

CHAPTER XIII

THE PRIMROSES

His metamorphosis took place in London without any help from me. After having his hair cut short, Felix changed from the costume of a French lady's maid into that of a young Russian gentleman; now at last I possessed a brother. This stranger, whom chance had thrown into my company during the sad days when my grief bordered on madness, showed me a sympathy that was none the less intelligent for being mute. He acted as children do when the grown people about them are mourning the death of a loved one; at such times very little boys are often professors of tact: not knowing just what to say, they say nothing at all, and in this way avoid being awkward in their manifestations of pity, at a time when no one else has the grace to be silent.

Felix consoled me by his presence, and by his presence alone. He never left me. It almost seemed that when he assumed Sasha's name, he had taken it upon himself to treat me as a sister. He sat beside me for hours; he held my hand and said nothing. Sometimes he had me look at Marie's picture; sometimes he pondered over it himself. At such moments I would try to describe the colors that the photograph could not render. I said, speaking as much to myself as to him:

"Her hair is blonde, but not pale, and it shines even in the darkness. It has a life of its own: each hair is a gleaming thread of gold that bends and does not break. Together they vibrate in the light, and you almost expect to hear them ring; she has Aeolian hair. Each golden thread is infinitely light, but the whole is heavy, heavy. . . ."

After a pause I said:

"Her cheeks are bright and cool. Even in the hot sunlight, some flowers keep their freshness. Her skin . . . have you ever touched camellias? Her eyes tell great truths—ah, no one knows how great! Her eyes tell all the truth; they are mournful eyes. Her lips are always smiling. What happy lips you have, Marie!"

I was using the present tense, for I refused to think of her as a corpse. The moment we speak in the past tense of something we love, we kill it in ourselves. "Marie *is* pink," I said to Felix.

From one of the three valises containing our family treasures and the relics of Gatchina, I took the snuff-box on which the Rose of St. Petersburg was painted in miniature. I wished to show Felix the color of her eyes, which were Marie's. He read the curious names and repeated them:

APHERIDON——ASTARTE

My new brother asked no questions; he always waited for me to speak. On one occasion he told me: "Treat me as your slave. I am little Felix Soltikov, your slave. I owe you my life, since it is because of you that I shall accomplish my mission. If you hadn't come to my aid, I should have been sent to a concentration camp, and the sentinels would have killed me the very first time I tried to escape."

When I took possession of his young imagination, I knew that I was not making him my own slave, but that of Marie. He was becoming the lover of a dead woman, and I felt no remorse. I knew that my sister lived on in my thoughts, my words, my gestures; I knew that as long as she lived, she would please; and it was only natural that she should be loved. Since Felix was there, he would be her first victim, and I felt no pity for him.

❧

Thanks to Gordon's influence, which had protected me since our arrival in England, we were able to leave London without difficulty; we embarked from Dover on April 5.

My one desire was to return to Biarritz. I wished to revisit the scene of my parting with Marie.

I told myself that one should be able to live with the thought of one's never again being young. Rarely, however, does it spring full-fledged into one's mind, as it did with me. Marie had been my own youth, discovered far too late

and lost too soon. I buried this youth within me;
I kept it embalmed in my heart.

If people can come and go, drink, eat, and
sleep with the knowledge that their better days
are gone forever, it is only because they can sum-
mon up the past. Henceforth I should live so that
Marie could live. It was my duty to become the
sad old woman I was destined to be, so that I
could give her radiant memory a dwelling place.
For this diamond to glitter, I should have to re-
sign myself to being its matrix of clay. To die
would be to forget her.

Gordon was waiting for me in Boulogne. He
was so visibly stirred at the sight of me that I
wondered whether the pain I caused him might
not be physically more than he could bear. While
Marie was living, he had scarcely noticed the resemblance between us, but it overwhelmed him
now that she was no longer there to hide me from
his eyes. Henceforth my whole family would
consist of Gordon; his life and mine were united
by the thousand bonds of grief.

My father was no more; Aunt Alix had taken my mother to the Swiss asylum where my sister Elizabeth was dragging out her life. Olga, at the mention of whose name I shivered, had been forced to leave France when the husband of her choice was expelled as an undesirable alien. The "convalescent home for wounded British and Russian officers" was quite empty at present, Fairfax and Frazer having disappeared like ghosts. After an absence of only five months, I was returning, the last of my family, to a deserted house. I was accompanied by two strangers, one of whom watched over me, while I was supposed to keep watch over the second.

Our old servants received me with silent pity. The housekeeper gave me a key, that of my old room, which no one had entered since Marie's death.

As head of the family, I was to occupy my mother's two rooms. They were crowded with portraits of Sasha at all his ages—of which he possessed so very few! Here he reigned alone;

yonder in the corner of the park, he now had a consort. Marie's young body had been placed above his, in the crypt of the little chapel, like a layer of new blossoms from an old tree, on a soil already strewn and enriched with the blossoms of former years.

Upstairs, in the story once reserved for the children, I heard the shutters creaking in the wind all night outside the empty room that had once been mine. I rose at dawn to put an end to the noise. In my bare feet, I entered the abandoned room, and found it flooded with morning light that poured in through a corner window facing the bed. I stopped, entranced by the beauty of the dawn. One other morning I had seen the same light bathing these walls: it was the morning of my ninth birthday, a few hours before the green parrot was given me and then snatched out of my hands. I had prayed all night, hoping to make myself worthy of the gift; better to resist sleep and temptation, I had drawn back the heavy curtains and knelt in the bright moonlight. The dawn had found me with open eyes, and had crowned me with roses on the morning that came so near to being my last. . . .

I went to the window overlooking the sea and flung it open. The great camellia bushes that grew in the shelter of a projecting ledge were dropping their petals one by one. The dark, glossy leaves still mirrored every blossom, but the flowers themselves were like white corpses stained with iodine.

I walked up to the glass where Marie and I had so often decomposed our faces. Taking a shawl that lay gathering dust on a chair, I covered the mirror, as Miss Grey had often done so many years before. Then, kneeling beside the bed where Marie had spent her last night on earth, I repeated her own words in a low voice:

"Don't be sorry if I'm not there, and pray for me. I *wished* to die."

*

It was high time for Felix to resume his lost identity. Gordon had undertaken to aid him, but with the war still raging and every one talking of

spies and counter-spies, the task proved even
more difficult than we had expected. The Englishman was writing a great many letters.
Armed with the answers he had received from
London and Paris, he set out for Bayonne to convince the military authorities that Sasha was
really not Sasha. The ship captains and bankers
who were expecting him in Hong Kong, in
Shanghai, in Tientsin, wished to be certain that
he was Felix Soltikov in person, and not Alexander Panine, before they carried him on their
vessels or gave him money from their vaults. The
proofs they required would have to be furnished
by the slow-moving administrative minds of the
Department of the Basses-Pyrénées. Stamps
would have to be affixed to documents that did
not yet exist; red tape would have to be wound,
unwound, rewound; and before certain acts
could be legalized, their illegality would have to
be officially established.

Ever since the Peace of Brest-Litovsk, the military authorities had been very distrustful of
Russians, and they showed no haste to deprive

me of the handsome young brother whom I had claimed on the strength of a false passport.

While Gordon was pleading his cause in Bayonne, Felix himself was scrupulously observing the instructions he had received: he was to accompany me wherever I went, and was never to leave me alone when Gordon was away. What did they think I would do? Could they not have seen that I was determined to live for Marie, who had ceased to live, and that I had no reason to die for her, because she was dead?

With Felix I visited all the scenes that reminded me of her birth and life. I took him to the Solitude of Anglet, where he shared in the perfect silence. We knelt in the hut, on the sand, before the curious statue of the Empress Eugénie dressed as the Madonna of the Seven Sorrows. We saw the grave-mounds of sand with their crosses of white shells. We sat among the yuccas, at the edge of the road, and I told him the story of the "lilies-of-the-valley for giants."

One afternoon I planned an excursion to the

villa of Calaouça, which our friend the Russian lady had sold long before. There it was that I first heard of my sister's birth. I wished to see the wall which borders the road, and drive through the gate, and stop at the great oak where we had watched for my father, whose mournful gesture had warned me from a distance that we mustn't be glad.

The road to the Basque house of Calaouça passed through a little wood called the Bois de Boulogne, from which one could see Lake Marion gleaming among the trees. At the top of the hill, I stopped the carriage and sent our old coachman to a farmhouse near by; he was to ask whether strangers were allowed to enter the villa.

I did not know how many times this lovely estate had changed hands during the last twenty years, nor who was its latest owner. We sat on the wooded slope that overlooks the lake; Felix had asked the coachman to be sure to ask what time it was. He had forgotten his watch, and doubtless he was afraid of being late, since Gordon had given us strict instructions to meet him in Bayonne before the local officials went home for the day.

We tried to guess at the time by looking at the sun. "Half-past two," I ventured, judging by its height and warmth. Felix held out his hand and stared at the shadow it cast on the dead leaves. "Or maybe three," he said. We spoke in hushed voices. A few miles away, in a place where the all-powerful sun never entered, Marie was sleeping, unmoved by all the charms of the weather. This lovely day was one of those she had destroyed for herself in her fever. I closed my eyes to be like her, to suppress the day. But I heard the birds singing; I breathed the air that was heavy with the perfume of the wood-flowers; I felt the heat and light beating through my closed eyelids. . . .

I opened them under the influence of the irresistible sun, just as the primroses and daisies were opening their yellow eyes all round me, watching. . . .

Felix's eyes seemed to be growing wider. His

face was very near to mine. He was pale. He bent forward as if about to fall. . . . I took his hand, thinking he was ill. Instantly a bright red covered his cheeks. A wave of purple invaded his forehead. . . . He made a sharp movement, and his hat, brushing against mine, fell to the ground. I felt that my blood was passing from my hand into his icy hand, was flowing to the roots of his hair; that he was colored by the beating of my heart. . . .

I ceased to see him.

It was then he kissed me.

CHAPTER XIV

THE STORY OF APHERIDON

AND ASTARTE

IT WAS a strange betrothal. . . .

". . . She is not dead, but sleepeth. *Talitha cumi*—Damsel, I say unto thee, arise."

It was a case of mistaken identity. The dead girl had risen, and since it is said in the Gospels that "something should be given her to eat," we nourished her with promises and falsehoods.

Marie came back to life at the touch of Felix. His kisses, his oaths of fidelity, were for her, and I received them with the deep incredulity one feels even in the most pleasant dreams. I abandoned myself to this one, knowing it was a dream and nothing more. I promised Felix everything he desired; his visionary glances frightened me; I had known other eyes that saw the nonexistent.

I swore to love him always and never to change. This was an easy promise, for he so resembled Sasha that I seemed to have loved him all my life. I adopted his opinions blindly and shared his hopes: we were to be married as soon as he had rescued the Czar. On his return from Asia, I would give him everything that was mine, except my age. . . .

❧

Six months after having adopted my brother's name, with the posthumous aid of my father, who had allowed him to take it, and of myself, who had helped him to bear it, the false Sasha was able to resume his own identity.

His mission was delayed, but not abandoned. The fate of the imperial family had aroused the most contradictory rumors. Felix left for China and Manchuria, hoping to reach Tobolsk, in December, 1918, after the signing of the armistice. Gordon and I accompanied him to Marseilles. I did not try to dissuade him from his project; I even urged him to accomplish it, feigning a patriotic loyalty I never felt. He would have to fulfill the promises he had made if my promises toward him were to be kept. His travels would last for months or years; perhaps he might forget me. By the power of circumstances, I had been forced to hope that he would!

A letter from Mme. Soltikov, received at the very moment of his departure, had destroyed the illusion into which I had fallen. Like a sleep-walker who hears his name spoken, I read her words and wakened from my dream.

At present the sea lay between us; I tried to imagine a vaster sea, an ocean so boundless that the distance between us became an insurmountable obstacle to our union, even in thought. . . .

Felix sent me a letter from Alexandria. "I love you," he said, "and when I write you, it is like walking on the sea."

❧

Gordon, still looking for ways to distract me, suggested a trip to Italy. This country is said to have the climate of happiness, and it attracts

204

those who suffer and those who love. Both classes imagine that joy is breathed in with the air.

I knew India and America, but I had never seen Venice. Since the plan of this city is such that there is no place for horses, and since its lagoon is unsuitable for a polo field, my husband had never included it in our itineraries.

Gordon had spent many years in Venice. He knew it, loved it, and had chosen it for me as a total change from everything I remembered. He took me to the Square of St. Mark to show me horses on the roof and pigeons on the ground; he led me through streets that had the animation of a theater lobby between the acts. They were crowded only with people; animals and machines were never admitted.

"One must be human to live here," he told me, "and this is the most human city left in the world. It is inhabited solely by people, and it is arranged like a fine dwelling: one hears only the sound of footsteps and conversations; the streets are hallways leading to magnificent and nobly furnished rooms; the public squares are ballrooms open to the sky; the churches are like carved sideboards standing against a wall of light."

He thought that I might choose this splendid mansion as a home. Tacitly he had decided not to leave me till the day of Felix's return. He wished to know where I would spend my life, and thought that I still seemed hesitant.

&

It was in Venice, one Saturday night, that I told Gordon my whole story. I had already made all arrangements to return to France the following day.

"Dear friend," I said with an effort, "I should like to tell you something that really can't be told, and at the same time I should prefer not to explain it too clearly, for there are mysteries which can be understood only by those who live them. Do you remember the day when you saw me crying after my visit to the medium? It was because she had read my heart.

"Where does Maria Serguyevna's story begin? Where does my mother's story begin? Where is

206

the end of my own story and Marie's? In reality, these stories are one and the same: they deal with a single love, an undying passion which has directed all our lives."

A few days before, he had given me a very old edition of Montesquieu's *Persian Letters*, and the book was lying before me as I spoke. I opened it to a page he had called to my attention, a page bearing a very familiar title on which his eyes had fallen with surprise and mine with horror: *The Story of Apheridon and Astarte*.

I read this little romance to Gordon from beginning to end. It tells how Apheridon the Persian had loved his sister from their earliest childhood; how he wished to marry her in accordance with the religious precepts of the Ghebers or Zoroastrians and against all the teachings of Mohammed; how he carried off Astarte at the risk of his life; and how, after losing her once more, he sold himself and his child by her as slaves in order to redeem her from bondage. . . .

I showed Gordon the lines I had first read in a letter from my great-grandmother to the hand-

some Alexander: "The first time I can embrace
you, my brother, I think I shall die in your
arms."

I told my only friend of my visit to Gatchina,
where I had discovered our own resemblance to
the Rose of St. Petersburg. I described the letters
she had exchanged with her brother under these
borrowed names, which, in my ignorance, I had
believed to be taken from some old romance of
chivalry. The book which had served as their
model must have been within reach of my hand,
for the library of Gatchina, like all old Russian
libraries, was crowded with French works of the
eighteenth century. Alexander Dalgorukin and
his Rose of St. Petersburg, insensible to Montesquieu's ironic attitude toward this incestuous
union, had loved each other as Ghebers. At present I realized that the story was theirs, ours, my
own. It was a sort of mirror in which I saw the
past and the future reflected simultaneously. The
past controlling the future, and the future repro-
ducing the past, I had only to look behind me in
order to see what was to come. I knew that the

brother and the sister would seek each other forever, having found each other once. Till the end
of time, and in spite of every obstacle, they
would strive to be reunited. I remembered the
stern rules of the Eastern Church, which pursues
and strikes with anathema even the superficial
likeness, even the shadow of such unions. Its
laws prohibit marriage between brothers-in-law
and sisters-in-law, between two brothers and two
sisters of different families, between the children
of brothers and sisters, and between the children
of their children, even to the third generation
and beyond!

My father and mother had broken one of these
commandments, and one that is always observed
in Russia. They had married in spite of being
first cousins, and we, their children, were twice
descended from Maria Serguyevna, their common grandmother. In their own eagerness to
have descendants, did they every think of the
ancestors they were giving us?

They had branded us at birth with the marks
of a passion that was older and stronger than our-

selves. What I now wished to tell Gordon was difficult to express. In me, as in Astarte, "love had dawned before reason." The demon I learned to call by Sasha's name had tormented me from my earliest childhood. An unpredictable accident, diphtheria, had deprived me of my brother, yet I had continued to search for him everywhere, throughout the whole of nature. When I was nine years old, my passion had been directed toward a bird that happened to light on my beaver muff. And I told Gordon the story of the green parrot. Detail for detail, it resembled the story of Marie, except that my sister's love had been wakened, not at nine, but at nineteen, and that it had killed her.

As a sort of antidote to the sorrow of losing the one she loved, an emotion too strong in all of us to be overcome, my mother had hoped intensely, and her hope had slowly transformed itself into madness. Marie had yielded at once, and I, being only a child, had resisted through weakness—at what a cost to myself! Under the influence of a violent shock, some people cling to life itself, but lose the power of speech. Such, in a way, had been my own experience. During all my youth I had been dumb, incapable of loving; I had been deaf to passion; and after bringing desires to life, I had watched them die in my presence like the great flocks of birds which, in the Greek fable, fell lifeless as they approached the infernal lake.

Involuntarily, I had given my husband more mistresses than he would ever have taken if he had remained unmarried and I a virgin. I had destroyed magnificent friendships, yet still I deemed myself innocent. I had sapped the foundations of ancient affections, and had created such a thirst for love in those about me that I became the direct, though unacknowledged, cause of several marriages—a service for which I received no thanks.

My weakness, which so many women mistook for an insolent superiority, did not arouse their sympathy; those who should have borne with my infirmity felt envious instead, for it cannot be denied that women regret their passion even when they are most deeply in love. And none of them had pitied me sincerely for being exempt from happiness.

My solitude, though it was envied by some and doubted by others, was none the less real. I had grown accustomed to my loneliness, and those who thought of sharing it with me had tired of it sooner than they expected. Others took their place, but only for a moment; expecting their love to be recompensed, they too carried their disappointment elsewhere. To be invincible is to be pacific, and the peace that reigned about me proved boring to men as soon as they lost their hope of destroying it.

My insensibility was questioned only during my travels. For the first few days after my arrival in new cities or new countries where my good reputation had not preceded me, I became a subject of gossip like other women. Old men ripe in experience would say of me:

"She will have her day!"

The young men thought:

"If she doesn't love me, it's only because she's incapable of love."

Each man considered himself preferable to all the others, and accordingly testified to my virtue:

"She refused me, so of course she wouldn't accept my brother or my friend."

Later they advanced much simpler explanations. My lover, whose name nobody could remember, had died under tragic circumstances. Others said that I had once been betrayed and had sworn never to love again.

I might easily have astonished the old or young men who gossiped about me by telling them that I had been cured of love by love itself. The one I loved had not betrayed me, nor had he died a tragic death. Besides, his infidelities mattered very little, since he was a bird, and he belonged to a species that lives for a hundred years. They would never have believed that I was immunized against passion, and I myself, who thought that I was, had proved to be mistaken.

If Marie had lived; if Renell Page had never

crossed her field of vision as the parrot had crossed my own path on the road to old St. Martin's; if she had seen Felix at the time when she was ready for love, she would not be dead, and she would have suffered the misfortune that had just attacked me after three generations. When I said, months before, that I was existing only for my sister, I had not realized the meaning that time would give to my words.

I told Gordon about the scene of the kiss, which had taken place just as the medium described it. When, in the little wood, the mysterious breath had passed over my face, it was Marie's youth and not my own that was reviving within me.

"Do you think," I said, "that Felix would have dared to kiss a woman as cold and self-restrained as I have always been—a woman who was ten years older than himself, and who treated him as a child? In reality, he was pursuing his dream of Marie . . . and he found her at last."

I thought of the words that Maria Serguyevna had repeated a hundred years before: "The first

214

time I can embrace you, my brother, I think I shall die in your arms."

On the day when Felix embraced me, I still was ignorant of our relationship, but I felt that something fatal was being accomplished. I now knew that he was my father's only son—at least his only living son. Mme. Soltikov, in the letter I received at Marseilles, had confessed the truth about Felix's parentage. She begged me to watch over him on his return from Siberia, if he ever returned. When she met me in Stockholm, she hadn't dared to tell me that he was my brother, partly because she had never seen me alone, and partly because she felt timid in my presence.

I told Gordon:

"You see, it's always Sasha! The life I have lived was not my own, but Maria Serguyevna's. Is one's body merely a haunted house? Must I give birth to the child that my mother tried vainly to create anew? Am I destined to perpetuate this blood? Let me say once and for all, dear friend, that I refuse. And I want you to tell Felix, when he returns from Siberia in six months or a year, that I am his sister, and that he is never to see me again."

❧

I was leaving Venice the following evening. At noon, as the crowds were streaming out of the churches, I received the following note from Gordon:

"I had quite a little trouble in finding what I wanted. It was sure to exist in a seaport, but unfortunately this is a day of rest, and every shop in Venice is closed and barricaded—even that of Signor Passerotto, the bird-fancier, who is spending his Sunday in the country like a London merchant.

"I succeeded, however, in conscripting a little army of his neighbors. If the good signor fails to return by sunset, my partisans have promised to batter down his door. Whatever happens, you can depend on seeing me at the station this evening with your green parrot."

CHAPTER XV

SISTERHOOD

ONE morning Mlle. Vignot burst into my room while I was still in bed. She had come from a suburb of Nantes, where at present she was teaching French literature in a boarding school kept by nuns. My invitation had reached her just before the Easter holidays, and she had hastened to accept it. She didn't know why I was sending for her, but in any case she was ready for my sake to do "the impossible," as she said in her letter.

She saw the cage as soon as she entered. Inside it, the green parrot sat preening himself.

"Why, here he is at last," she said. "I'm so glad you have him. . . . He—he'll be a consolation for you."

"Dear Vignot, it isn't my nature to be consoled. Think of my mother; think of Marie. I love my bird, but he came to me too late, by a trick of destiny. His name is Nevermore."

I paused, while the bird cried harshly to welcome this early guest.

"He can talk in three languages, and he is yours, dear Vignot. I am retiring from the world, and I want to leave you my green parrot. Immoderate souls like mine and Marie's must choose between death and the cloister; we can find no refuge except in God.

"Should you like to know where I'm going? Out of France . . . yet I shall continue to live in the moral climate of your country, for you instilled French tastes in me during my childhood. After twenty, one can't become a Bernardine. And besides, the Solitude of Anglet is peopled with too many of my memories. I was having all sorts of difficulty about choosing a retreat, when one morning I received a sort of pious prospectus addressed to my mother by some one whose name I never heard. Our family, so it appeared from the letter, had promised a contribution to the French

Mission of Madura. I read on absent-mindedly,
but one or two phrases caught my attention, and
suddenly I felt like an undecided tourist who has
chosen a destination on the spur of the moment,
after musing over the posters in a railway station.
Here are the words that brought a picture to my
mind. . . . Listen!"

I had drawn a torn envelope from under the
pillow.

"The Mission of Madura, in the diocese of
Trichinopoli, is entrusted to the Fathers of the
Company of Jesus. It lies in the extreme south of
India, where, over an area of 17,249 square
miles, it ministers to the spiritual needs of some
280,000 Catholics. . . .

"Madura is a time-honored field for missionary work. St. Francis Xavier evangelized the
Fishery Coast and the neighboring state of Tra-
vancore. The Venerable de Britto was martyred
in Marava.

"After being reconstituted in 1836 by four
French Jesuits, the Mission, during its eighty-

two years of active existence, has claimed the lives of more than two hundred and forty missionaries.

"We are calling on apostolic souls and on generous benefactors everywhere to aid the Harvest of Souls, the Sisters of Our Lady of Sorrows, the Sisters of St. Anne, and all the holy women who are toiling in the vineyard. . . . Dowry of a missionary sister: 500 francs. Cost of building a chapel of earth and branches: 600 francs. . . ."

A sort of preëstablished harmony existed between what I was and what I was about to become: a sister. I had been a sister all my life: first that of Sasha, then that of Marie, and finally that of little Felix Soltikov.

To Mlle. Vignot I repeated the story I had told Gordon in Venice. I had asked her to come for a special purpose: I wished her to take charge of the fortune that remained to me, and to save it for Felix. All I intended to keep was my dowry as a nun, and six hundred francs for a chapel of earth and branches.

"You are wrong to cry, dear, good Vignot," I

said. "You are saving my life once more. I was a little Russian savage, and you taught me discipline; you gave me a French education. If you had been there to take Marie in your arms as you once took me, the day I lost my love, perhaps you would have rescued her from the anarchy of self-destruction. But you had been separated from her by Olga, who was destined to become the instrument of her destruction. As for me, I shall do as people did in the seventeenth century when they lost the wish to live: I shall take the veil, after having seen the side of life that is seen by impractical creatures like me, who give their hearts but once.

"Remember your own lessons and their influence on my childhood. Didn't you teach me to admire what Mlle. de Montpensier wrote when her friend Mlle. de Soissons became a Carmelite?—'She knew the world and despised it; this is what makes good nuns.'

"Do you think I could wait for Felix's death or his return? Could I be like the unhappy lovers of Gatchina and find an excuse for incest in the laws of Cambyses as invented by Montesquieu? Don't forget that if Felix loved me, it was only because he took me for another. I shall always have courage enough to resist a passion of which I feel I am not the real object. No, I shall go to Madura and practice renunciation in a chapel of earth and branches. Everything in me adheres and consents to this decision that was present in my spirit long before it took shape in my conscious mind. To die would not be enough: I wish to enjoy the spectacle of my death."

THE END